THE PLAGUE PIT

'Tom!' Jack yelled. He jumped down into the pit as his brother disappeared under the avalanche of dirt.

A hideous stench billowed out from the fallen cellar wall, and along with the sluice of slime, came something even more horrible.

Frankie let out a scream. The crawling slime bore with it an appalling burden. Spewing out with the mud was a whole mass of bones and skulls that turned and rolled and wheeled in the disgusting soup.

And the skulls were not animal skulls.

They were human skulls.

Books available in the DARK PATHS series

DARK PATHS
The Plague Pit

Allan Frewin Jones

MACMILLAN CHILDREN'S BOOKS

Created by
Allan Frewin Jones and Lesley Pollinger

Thanks to
Leigh Pollinger and Rob Rudderham

First published 1998 by Macmillan Children's Books
a division of Macmillan Publishers Limited
25 Eccleston Place, London SW1W 9NF
and Basingstoke

Associated companies throughout the world

ISBN 0 330 36807 9

1 3 5 7 9 8 6 4 2

A CIP catalogue record for this book is available from
the British Library.

Phototypeset by Intype London Ltd
Printed and bound in Great Britain by Mackays of Chatham plc, Kent

Contents

CHAPTER ONE

In Foul Places
Underground

'Well, this has to be just about the most disgusting smell I've ever encountered in my entire life!' Regan Vanderlinden's voice was squeaky and pinched. She was holding her nose between finger and thumb.

'Don't be such a wimp!' Tom Christmas said from behind her on the staircase. 'Get a move on. You're blocking the way.' Then he got a whiff of the cellar. 'Ewww!' He clamped his hand over his face. For once he had to agree with his American friend – the place smelled bad.

'What is *that*?' Frankie Fitzgerald gasped in shock as the stench hit her. 'How can anyone in their right mind work down here?'

Jack Christmas, Tom's older brother, was the last of the four friends on the stone stairway down to the cellar. The unpleasant smell came wafting up to him. 'No one said archaeology was all sunshine and roses.' He let out a choke of laughter. 'But this is a bit much! Anyone got a gas mask?'

A figure rose from behind a long hump of earth

down in the belly of the cellar. A young woman with short blonde hair, bright blue eyes and a broad, cheerful face. She was wearing grimy old clothes. Her face was smeared with dirt. She grinned.

'Hello, there!' she called up to them. 'You must be Darryl's friends.'

'I guess we must,' said Regan, still clinging on to her nose. 'Are you Rhea?'

'Spot on!' said the young woman. Jack guessed she must be in her late teens. 'You might find it stinks a bit down here,' she added, unnecessarily.

'You think?' said Regan.

Rhea's broad, toothy grin widened. 'Oh. You've noticed. Sorry, I suppose I should have warned you. Come on down, if you can stand it.'

The friends filed down into the cellar. All four of them were wearing rain-proof coats. It was a hot, sultry August day, but up above, a flash storm was sending the streets swimming. Their hair was dripping into their eyes and they left a wet trail as they descended the staircase. They'd been glad to get out of the pelting rain. Until they hit that smell.

The cellar was an unremarkable room with raw brick walls. It was underneath a row of large, grimy Victorian terraced buildings. They could see the boards of the floor above through the heavy beams of the ceiling. Shrouded in cobwebs and old grime. The ground was concrete, but an entire half of the concrete had been removed and the level there was now about a metre lower than the rest of the room. A big pile of oozy, black earth was heaped against one wall.

'Don't worry,' said Rhea. 'You'll get used to the

smell. After a bit you'll hardly notice it at all. How much has Darryl told you so far?'

'Dot buch,' Tom said, hanging tightly on to his nose.

Rhea was referring to Darryl Pepper, an eccentric young man in his late teens whom the four members of St Columb's School Archaeology Club had befriended.

ACE – the archaeology club – was run by a teacher, Mrs Tinker. Darryl was an ex-member and former St Columb student. His continuing passion for archaeology had led Jack, Tom, Frankie and Regan to him, despite the fact that he was seldom now in contact with the club. Mrs Tinker thought that some of Darryl's opinions had become just a little too strange since he'd left the school.

The four friends thought so too, but they had reason to believe that strange wasn't necessarily wrong. Not that they were crazy enough to say as much to Mrs Tinker. Their relationship with Darryl was strictly off-the-record so far as the school club was concerned.

A few days back, Darryl had told Frankie about an interesting dig that was going on in their own town. In Lychford itself. The local university was in control and, as usual, they were doing their best to keep a lid on everything until the work was finished. As the four friends knew, one of the problems that regularly troubled archaeological sites was amateurs with big, clumsy feet and metal detectors. All too often, valuable finds had been ruined or even carried off by people who didn't know any better – or who did know better but couldn't care less.

A whisper of Roman coins, for instance and those

3

people would be circling like vultures, waiting for the official dig to close down for the night so that they could move in.

Not that this particular site seemed likely to produce anything so romantic as Roman coins. It was under a modern factory and dated back to medieval times. It was a tannery. It had come to light when drains were being repaired. Darryl had found out about it through his friend Rhea Peake, an archaeology student working on the dig.

He had mentioned that Frankie and her friends would be interested in a visit. Rhea was convinced that Professor Paulson, who was in charge of the dig, would refuse access to visitors. So, Rhea had agreed to give the four friends a sneak-preview, as it were, on a Saturday morning when the dig would not normally be active.

And here they were, staring down into the black pit and wishing they'd left their noses upstairs in the rain.

'OK,' said Rhea, assuming that Tom's 'dot buch' meant that Darryl had left it to her to supply the details. 'Let me fill you in on what we know so far. For a start, do you all know what a tannery is?'

'It's a place where animal hides are turned into leather, isn't it?' said Frankie. She'd been doing some research on her home computer.

'That's right,' said Rhea. 'We think this place was active around about the thirteenth or fourteenth century.'

'Excuse me,' said Tom. 'Why is it so far under the ground? Did they always put these places right underground, or what?'

'It wouldn't have been underground at the time,'

4

said Jack. 'The ground level would have built up over the centuries.' Thirteen-year-old Jack was the more interested of the two brothers in archaeology. At the beginning, his twelve-year-old brother had only come along to the ACE meetings because the two of them always did everything together. But recent events had convinced Tom that archaeology certainly wasn't the dry, boring subject he would have imagined. Not by a long way!

'Yes, that's perfectly right,' said Rhea. 'Rubbish would be dumped out the back of people's houses, and this rubbish would slowly build up over hundreds of years. There were no refuse collections in those days.' She smiled. 'You just lobbed your junk out of the back window! And then the ground might fall into disuse for whatever reason until someone new came along and demolished what was left and built all over again. It's called stratification. And of course, as the modern level of the ground gradually rises, so the older remains sink lower and lower.' She gave them an anxious grin. 'Sorry, am I explaining this at all clearly?'

'Perfectly,' said Frankie. She looked up at the dark rafters. 'So, this building was built on the ruins of the tannery, right?'

'Well, possibly,' said Rhea. 'But there's a big gap between the fourteenth century and the late nineteenth century, when this building was put up. There could have been several other structures here in the interim. Professor Paulson is checking into old surveys of the area.'

'So, what have you found?' asked Regan. She peered into the levelled-out black hole in which

Rhea was standing. 'It looks kind of nasty and gooey to me.'

'It is,' said Rhea. 'Very. The soil in tanneries is generally black and sticky like this. We've found the kind of stuff you'd expect: cattle feet and horns. There wouldn't be any other bones normally; the butchers would have taken them out before sending the hides here. The hides would be brought to the tannery, tied by the feet to long poles.' Rhea gave them an amused look. 'Do you want me to go into the whole process? It's a bit yucky.'

'Go right ahead,' said Frankie. 'We can handle yucky.'

'OK, you asked for it,' said Rhea. 'First the hides would be washed clean of blood and dung and the salt used in the butchery process. This would usually be done down at a local stream.'

'Oh, nice,' said Regan. 'Well hygienic, huh?'

'I suppose you'd have done it in the kitchen sink,' said Tom.

'No,' said Regan. 'I wouldn't have done it at all. I'd have used plastic instead of leather.'

Tom stared at her. 'That's just totally ridiculous. Plastic wasn't invented for hundreds of years after this!'

'Yeah, right,' said Regan. 'But only because they were too busy messing around with leather, see? If they'd quit it with the leather, I figure someone would have invented plastic a whole lot sooner.'

'You're potty!' said Tom. 'I've never head such a load of—'

'Tom,' interrupted Jack. 'She's having you on.'

Regan grinned. Tom glared at her. She was always doing that. And he always fell for it. It was so annoying. She was a whole year younger than him, but she was forever out-gunning him like that. Pest!

'Take no notice of them, Rhea,' said Frankie. 'They're always like this. They love each other, really.'

'Get lost!' yelled Tom, and:

'No way!' Regan howled at the same time.

'Can we let Rhea finish?' suggested Jack. He looked at the young woman. 'So? They washed the hides down at the local stream. Then what happened?'

The four friends couldn't understand why Rhea was grinning so broadly – until she started her explanation. 'Once they'd been cleaned, the hides would be sprinkled with urine to help loosen the hair.'

'Excuse me,' Regan said, holding up both of her hands, the index finger extended on each. 'Did I just hear right?'

Rhea laughed. 'Yes.'

Regan closed her eyes and shuddered. 'Fine. OK. Right. I can live with that thought – just about. Carry on.'

'The hair would be scraped off,' Rhea continued. 'Then the hides would be immersed into a vat of warm dog dung or bird droppings, or into a bath of fermented barley or rye with stale beer or urine as the extra, magic ingredient.'

Tom exploded with laughter.

'If you think the place smells bad now,' said Rhea, 'imagine what it must have been like when it was in full swing.'

'I'd rather not,' said Frankie. 'Didn't people complain?'

7

'They certainly did,' said Rhea. 'Long and loud, if the existing records are anything to go by.'

'I don't blame them,' said Jack. 'Um, I know this is probably a silly question, but where did they get all the ur—'

'I don't think we need to go into all that,' Frankie said quickly. 'What happened next, Rhea?'

'Oh, various washing and preparation stages. These would take about a year. Then the hides could be sent for final curing. After which the leather was ready to be turned into shoes or whatever.' She turned and pointed to the far wall of the dig. 'Over there you can see the outlet for the old water supply. Tanneries needed plenty of water.' They followed the line of her finger. At about waist-height, the broken rim of a pipe jutted from the black soil.

'Excuse me again,' said Regan. 'Dumb question, I'm sure, but if all you're expecting to find is ooze and cow feet and horns and stuff like that, uh, what exactly is the point of grubbing around down here? I only ask because, like, I think archaeology is really neat, right? But I can't figure this out at all.'

'It's all useful info, isn't it, Rhea?' said Tom, hoping to get one ahead of Regan. 'Every site is different.' He remembered something Mrs Tinker had said. 'Every site has its own unique story to tell, right?'

'That's perfectly true,' said Rhea. 'Every piece of the jigsaw is useful, if only to confirm something that was already assumed.'

'Can I come down and have a closer look?' asked Tom. He was on a roll now. It was usually Regan who jumped into everything first. But this was one time when she wasn't going to beat him to it.

He looked challengingly at her. 'Coming?'

'Yeah, like I really need to squooge around hip deep in black slime,' said Regan. 'You're welcome to it.'

'Huh! Wimp.' Tom circled the pit until he came to the place where the earth had been left to form a steep ramp. He looked back at Jack and Frankie. 'Anyone else interested?'

'Um, no,' said Frankie, eyeing the ooze dubiously. 'You have a good look around down there for us, Tom, and then you can tell us all about it.'

'Pathetic, aren't they?' Tom said to Rhea. 'Afraid of getting a bit – urrk! Oh, yuck!' He stepped into wet mud that oozed up over his ankles and poured, thick and cold into his shoes. Too late he noticed that Rhea was wearing wellington boots.

Jack laughed. 'Mum will love you!' he said.

Biting her lips to stop from laughing, Rhea helped Tom to a less boggy area. 'It's getting worse down here,' she said. 'It must be seepage from all the rain. The chances are that some of the old drains are still in place. They're probably channelling the rain water down here. I hope it doesn't get too much wetter, or we'll be needing ladles instead of trowels.'

'Or snorkels,' said Frankie. 'Hey – maybe when you've finished, you could turn it into an underground swimming pool.'

Regan came closer to the broken edge of the remains of the concrete floor. She looked down into the black hole. 'Well?' she asked Tom. 'How's it going down there, huh? Enjoying yourself?'

Tom ignored her. He squelched over to the ragged crown of pipe that Rhea had shown them. A trickle of brown water ran down the earth wall. The smell was almost overpowering, but he was determined not to be put off by it.

He crouched, peering into the pipe. He imagined he must look just like a real archaeologist. Now all he needed was to say something clever – some throwaway comment to prove he knew everything there was to know about medieval tanneries.

'OK,' he said to Rhea. 'The water comes down this pipe, right? And it pours into the vats where the hides would be . . .' He stopped.

There was a strange noise coming down the pipe.

He peered into the black hole. The noise was getting louder.

He opened his mouth to speak.

'Er, I think maybe—' A flood of dark brown water came gushing out of the pipe right into his face. He was bowled off his feet, his mouth, nostrils, eyes and ears filled with the filthy deluge.

And as he floundered in the black muck, he heard a piercing shriek of laughter from above him.

It was Regan. Of course!

Tom spluttered and coughed, kicking his feet and windmilling his arms as he struggled to get clear. Rhea grabbed hold of his collar and dragged him out from under the spout of dirty water.

'Oh, Tom!' exclaimed Frankie. 'You twit!'

Tom stumbled to his feet. He was coated with the black slime and dripping with filthy, stinking water. He blinked, the whites of his eyes showing bright in the mudbath of his face.

'Gaaahhh!' he croaked. 'I . . . urrgh . . . gaahhh . . .'

Regan could hardly speak for laughing. 'Looking

good, Tom!' she wheezed, bent almost double above him. 'Who said archaeology wasn't glamorous?'

'It's not funny,' said Jack. 'Look at the state he's got himself in.'

Now that she'd rescued him from the lessening discharge of water, Rhea was standing back from him, her hand clamped over her mouth, her eyes boggling at the mess he was in. He looked and smelled like a walking sewage farm.

Tom wasn't just mired and foul and bedraggled – he felt totally stupid too. It was all Regan's fault! If he hadn't needed to show off in front of her, this would never have happened.

In a sudden eruption of anger, he squelched over to the wall and gave it as hard a kick as he could manage. As if his humiliation was the wall's fault.

The effect was a lot more dramatic than he'd expected.

His wild kick must have loosened some fragile thing that was holding the wall together. The entire structure suddenly belled out towards him. He gaped, frozen with shock. For a split second the wall hung over him like a bloated belly, then cracks appeared and spread and big chunks of black earth began to fall away. There was a rush and a crush and a slurry of loose mud and black slime that swept Tom off his feet.

'Tom!' Jack yelled. He ran forwards and jumped down into the pit even as his brother was inundated by the avalanche of dirt.

A hideous stench billowed out from the fallen wall, and along with the sluice of slime, came something even more horrible.

Frankie let out a scream. The crawling slime bore

with it an appalling burden. Spewing out with the mud was a whole mass of bones and skulls that turned and rolled and wheeled in the disgusting soup.

And the skulls were not animal skulls.

They were human skulls.

Dozens of them, vomited out on the lava of black slime beneath which Tom had now completely disappeared.

CHAPTER TWO
The Sickness Spreads

Tom awoke out of a black nightmare of grotesquely dancing skeletons and creeping brown mud and an unspeakable stench.

He was unbearably hot, but a chill rested on his forehead and the sweat that ran into his hair burned like ice.

He was lying down. Something lay sprawled across him, like a dead animal, making it difficult for him to move. The world spun, black and troubled behind his eyelids, rimmed with red fire. He felt sick.

'Jack . . .?' It was a croak. He didn't recognize the broken noise as his own voice. He cracked an eyelid open.

He was staring up at a pock-marked ceiling, shrouded in swarming gloom. He tried to lift an arm but the pressure on him made it impossible. The action drained the strength out of him. He licked his lips, but his tongue felt as dry as sandpaper.

A vile smell tormented him. He turned his head this way and that, as if to try and escape the smell;

as if the smell was a thick, noxious liquid and he was beneath it, desperately seeking fresh air.

The place he was in began to come clear to him, like something rising out of a night fog. It was a long, dark room – a hall. Pale oblongs of grey light striped the smoky walls: tall windows through which bled a sickly effulgence. There were black beams. And there were low shapes. Rows of long dark low shapes.

Indistinct figures glided purposefully through the mist.

Tom heard coughing and moaning.

He tried again to sit up, but the weight held him down.

He screwed up his eyes. Something seemed to be squatting on his chest. A gibbous shape, heavy as lead, formless as a black cloud. A flat, broad face turned to him and a wide, cavernous mouth grinned a splintered grin. Red eyes gleamed.

Tom cried out and struggled wildly.

Something laughed.

One of the circling shapes broke out of the slow swirl of fog and moved towards him.

Tom stared at it. It seemed to billow as it neared him, its edges wavering and dissolving. He couldn't focus on it. Sweat poured off him.

The black thing loomed over him. A sickly-sweet smell rained down on him. The thing was a great black bird with a long sharp beak. A monstrous bird. The tip of the huge, heavy beak dipped over his heart.

He felt he would be impaled on that beak. He screwed his eyes closed and waited for the death blow.

*

'Mrs Christmas? I think he's with us.' The voice sounded clear as a bell through the raven fog. Tom opened his eyes. A face swam into view above him. A smiling face, lined and cragged and topped with a fuzz of iron-grey hair.

The face hovered in a cloud of brilliant white light.

'Tom?' A second face floated into sight.

'Mum?' Tom felt weak. Terribly weak. And he felt sick. And his head throbbed. But at least he was out of that other place. That other dreadful place.

His mother took his hand. She smiled and he could see the anxiety brimming in her eyes.

'You had us worried there for a bit.' Tom blinked as his father's face emerged from the light. His other hand was grasped. 'I know mud baths are meant to be good for the complexion, but there *are* limits, you know.'

Tom attempted a weak grin. 'Where's Jack?'

'Right here.'

Tom lifted his head from the pillow. Jack was standing at the foot of the bed. He grinned and wiped his arm across his forehead in a comic gesture of relief.

'What happened?' Tom asked.

'Don't you remember?' asked Jack.

'I remember . . . a . . . big bird . . . a crow . . . or something . . .'

Fretful faces turned to the man.

'He's still a bit out of it,' said the man. 'It'll take a few minutes, I expect. Don't worry about it.' The man leaned a little closer to Tom. 'Tom? I'm Dr Fairfax. Do you know where you are?'

'Oakhurst Grove?'

'That's where we lived before we moved to Lychford,' said Mrs Christmas. 'Tom? We don't live in Bannerton any more, darling. We live in Lychford now. We've been here for a couple of months. Don't you remember?'

The bright light resolved itself into a small, clinically bright hospital room.

'Oh!' He looked around, his eyes focused at last. 'I got covered in a load of stinky gunge. It was all Regan's fault.'

Tom's mother and father looked at Jack.

He shook his head. 'Regan wasn't anywhere near him.'

'I don't mean she *did* it,' said Tom. Shivering weakness sang a sleepy song through his body. 'I meant she ... oh, never mind.' He closed his eyes. 'I can still smell it,' he murmured. 'Pooh!'

He slept.

Jack looked up from his book at a sound from the bed. Tom was awake.

'Hello, again,' said Jack. 'Feeling better?'

Tom lifted a heavy hand to claw the sleep out of his eyes. Jack was sitting beside the bed. The book was open in his hand. An angle-poise illuminated the pages. Venetian blinds were drawn across blue twilight.

'Yes,' Tom said. He struggled to sit up. It was too much effort. 'No,' he groaned. 'I feel like death warmed up. Where's Mum and Dad?'

'They've gone to get you some pyjamas and stuff,' said Jack. 'They'll be back soon. Are you hungry? Or thirsty?'

'Thirsty. Yes.'

Jack poured Tom a glass of water from a jug on the bedside table. It took all of Tom's strength to hold the glass to his lips.

'Why do I feel so bad?' he asked.

'How much do you remember?' asked Jack.

'Oh, I remember the whole thing,' said Tom. He smiled. 'Why? Does everyone think I've lost my memory? Did I get a bash on the head or something?' He frowned. 'My head does ache a bit – but then everything seems to be aching right now. Right down to my toenails. I suppose that's what comes of having a wall fall on you. Jack?'

'What?'

'Remind me not to do that again – whatever I did that made the wall fall in on me. If I ever look like I'm about to do it again, remind me not to. I feel sick.'

'Shall I fetch a nurse?'

'No.'

'Rhea feels really bad about what happened,' said Jack.

'I should hope she does,' said Tom. 'Inviting people down there to get squashed by walls. Charming!'

'It wasn't her fault.'

'When can I go home?'

'Not just yet.'

Tom peered towards the window. 'But it's nearly night time.'

'I know. They want to keep you in overnight for observation. Dr Fairfax is a bit bothered about all that filthy water you swallowed. He thinks you might have swallowed some germs along with it.'

'I should think I *did*,' said Tom. 'About ten gallons of germs! I bet Regan is laughing her socks off about this.'

'Hardly,' said Jack. 'She was as freaked as the rest of us when you went down under all that gunk.' Jack looked at his brother. 'Do you remember much about that?'

'I remember seeing it coming down. And I remember thinking, oops, bad move.' He frowned, raking his brain, but the memories cut off with the collapse of the wall. 'Nope,' he said. 'Nothing after that.'

'I dragged you out from under the heap of dirt,' said Jack. 'You were out of it – completely. Rhea dashed off to call an ambulance. Frankie did some first aid stuff on you. She was brilliant. And so was Regan.'

Tom gave his brother a worried look. 'They didn't give me the kiss of life, did they?'

'No. Nothing like that.'

'Phew! Thank heavens!'

'They made sure you were breathing OK,' Jack said, laughing softly at Tom's squeamishness. 'And then we carried you up out of the hole and Frankie put you in the recovery position. The ambulance took about . . . oh . . . fifteen minutes, I suppose.' Jack smiled. 'It seemed like ages at the time. Then you woke up a couple of hours later saying it was all Regan's fault and talking about big crows, or some such gibberish.' Jack laughed. 'Dr Fairfax was worried that you'd gone barmy until I explained that you're always like that when you first wake up.'

'A crow . . .' murmured Tom. A faint, dark

memory stirred. 'A big black crow . . . yes. And . . .' The memory flicked out of sight around a corner of his mind.

Jack looked at him. 'Do you remember anything else about when the wall collapsed?' he asked cautiously.

'I . . . remember . . . bones!' Tom's eyes widened. He stared at Jack. 'When the wall fell – all the earth was full of – bones.' He frowned at his brother. 'But Rhea said there wouldn't be bones. She said just hooves and horns, didn't she?'

Jack looked carefully at his brother. Was this a good time to tell him?

Tom's eyebrows knitted. 'What?' he said sharply. He could see something in Jack's wide-spaced, clear brown eyes.

'They weren't animal bones, Tom,' said Jack. 'I know you're going to hate this, but they were human bones. Rhea thinks the tannery must have been right next to some old graveyard that everyone had forgotten about.'

Jack expected his brother to react with revulsion, but it wasn't disgust that ignited in Tom's horror-struck eyes, it was a ghastly realization. He reached out and gripped Jack's wrist. Sweat beaded on his forehead and his eyes looked feverish. He lifted his head.

'That's not right,' he whispered hoarsely. 'It wasn't an ordinary graveyard, Jack. It wasn't ordinary at all. It was a mass grave. It was full of people who died of the plague.'

'Don't be daft,' Jack said uneasily. 'What on earth makes you think that?'

Tom's head fell back on the pillows.

'I don't know,' he said, his voice shaking. He turned his head and his burning eyes stared into his brother's face. 'Jack?' he whispered. 'Have I got the plague?'

CHAPTER THREE
Vinegar with Everything

Regan sat bolt upright in bed. Morning light seeped into her bedroom through thick velvet curtains. It had taken her a complete change of clothes and half an hour under the shower yesterday evening to get the stink of that cellar out of her nostrils. And now what could she smell?

'Vinegar!' she said aloud. 'What the heck is going on around here? I smell *vinegar*!'

She slipped out of bed and prowled the large room, sniffing. The smell was gone again. She sniffed the bedcovers. No, nothing. She marched over to the window and pulled the heavy curtains open.

Her bedroom overlooked the huge, professionally tended gardens of the vast house that her parents were renting. She could never figure why her folks lived in such big places: her mom spent most of the week up in London doing her diplomacy stuff with Ministers of State and foreign dignitaries. And her dad was either in Dubai or Kuala Lumpur or St

Petersburg or on a jet plane zipping off to lord knows where else.

Regan was used to being dumped in some grand house by her folks and then left to her own devices. She often wondered what it must be like to have parents who were all over you all the time. Not good, she'd decided, some years ago. The way things worked in her family, the only person she needed to take any account of was the au pair, and Jennie – the latest – had bimbo written right through her.

Regan pulled on some clothes. Black. Her favourite colour. She took a quick look at herself in the mirror. Her poker-straight, jet-black hair was centre-parted and hung down way past her shoulders. Her eyes were a startling blue in her pale, broad face.

She winked at herself. 'Looking good, kid!'

She opened her bedroom window and sucked in some fresh air. Hot. Even this early in the day, the air was still and hot. Lychford had been like an oven for the past two weeks. Yesterday's stormclouds were lumbering slowly away and there were ragged patches of electric blue up there.

Regan had been born in upstate New York, but all her life she'd been hauled about from one country to another by her rich and influential parents. Lychford was the first place she had ever felt at home. She couldn't explain it – that was just the way she felt. With any luck, her folks would quit orbiting the world for a while and she'd be able to grow a few roots here.

She headed downstairs to the kitchen.

She heard Jennie's voice, like fingernails down a blackboard.

' . . . so, anyway, I was, like, excuse me, but I don't see any no-parking signs around here. And he says, like, no one parks on a zebra crossing . . .'

Regan took a deep breath and continued down the stairs. Jennie was on the phone. Jennie was always on the phone – to her boyfriend in California. Brad.
' . . . huh? Yeah, a *zebra* crossing. That's what they call a pedestrian walkway over here. Huh? Yeah! Totally crazy! And they have *no* valet parking, would you believe.' Regan walked into the kitchen. Jennie was perched on the table. She was as thin as a rake and as blonde as sulphuric acid. The mobile phone was tucked under her chin and she was busy painting her nails silver while she was talking.
' . . . uh-huh. I had to park the car myself. I mean, is this country backward, or what?' She gave Regan a disinterested look. 'Just a moment, Brad.' She dispatched a cheesy, insincere smile. 'Hi, there, Regan. I'm just talking with Brad.'

'Really? I'm stunned.' Regan marched over to the fridge. 'What about breakfast?'

'I've already eaten, thanks,' said Jennie. That hadn't been quite what Regan had meant. One day, Jennie would fix some food and Regan would just drop dead of shock.

She opened the fridge. The smell of vinegar wafted out.

'Ew! What?' She slammed the door. 'What have you been doing around here?' she demanded. 'The whole place reeks!'

Jennie sniffed. 'I don't smell anything,' she said.

Regan stared at her. 'You're kidding?'

Jennie took another sniff and shook her head.

'Nope, nothing.' She smiled. 'Perhaps someone around here needs to take a shower?'

'I'm not smelling *me*,' Regan said in exasperation. 'It's vinegar. Everything stinks of vinegar. What's wrong with you? Has your nose gone on vacation along with your brain?'

'Well, excuse *me*, Little Miss Bad-Hair-Day, but I don't have to put up with *that* kind of talk! I'm out of here!' She slid off the table and stalked out. 'Brad?' Regan heard as Jenny departed. 'Yeah. I'm back.' Giggle. 'No, it was nothing at all. Just *Regan*. What was I talking about?'

Regan dismissed Jennie from her mind.

Vinegar! What was it with the *vinegar*?

She shook her head. Baffled. Maybe that awful smell yesterday had ruined her nose for all time.

Regan poured herself a glass of orange juice. It smelled of vinegar. She tipped it down the sink. She began to think about the implications of spending the rest of her life imagining that everything smelled of vinegar.

The phone rang out in the hall. She let it ring a few times, just to see if Jennie would pick up. She didn't.

It was Frankie.

'Hiya,' said Regan, settling down on the stairs. 'Is your nose working OK?'

'I'm sorry?'

'I keep smelling vinegar,' Regan explained. 'It's driving me crazy. I just wondered if you were having the same problem.'

'Er, no,' said Frankie. 'Jack just phoned me.'

'Is everything OK with Tom?' Regan couldn't keep the anxiety out of her voice. Seeing him go down under that avalanche of muck and bones had been one of the most terrifying experiences of her entire life.

'Well, yeah, up to a point, said Frankie. 'They kept him in the hospital overnight.'

'I guess that makes sense,' said Regan. 'He sure was one big mess when we fished him outta there. Do they think he has some disease?'

'I expect they're just being careful,' said Frankie.

'I guess.' Regan thought for a moment. 'Can't you get tetanus from dirty water?'

'I thought that was from rusty nails,' said Frankie. 'Anyway, I'm sure he hasn't got anything at all. They're just being hyper-careful.'

'Yeah, I can see that,' said Regan. 'They wouldn't want to risk a major lawsuit cos they released him when he had something terminal.'

'Regan! You've got the most morbid mind, sometimes. Tom hasn't got anything wrong with him. Trust me. He'll be fine.'

A smell wafted past Regan. She sniffed. Vinegar again!

'Anyway,' Frankie continued. 'I just phoned to see if you fancy coming to the hospital with me later on this morning? I was thinking of going over there around midday, if that suits you.'

'Yeah, sure,' Regan said, sniffing the phone to check the smell wasn't coming from there. 'Are you sure he'll still be there? They might have discharged him by then.'

'No, they won't,' said Frankie. 'Jack said he'll be in there for at least another couple of days.'

'A couple of *days*,' said Regan. 'It doesn't sound

to me like there's nothing wrong with him. You don't keep people in hospital for two days unless—'

'Regan! Can we not talk about this, please?'

'Oh. Yeah. OK. I was only saying—'

'I know what you were saying,' said Frankie. 'I'd really rather not have to think about it, OK?'

'Yeah, but—'

'Regan, I'm worried, OK? And you're not helping!'

'Oh. Sorry.' Regan remembered something about Frankie. It came bombing into the front of her brain like a crashing plane. Frankie's mother had died in hospital. Sure, Frankie had only been two at the time, so she couldn't have known a whole lot about it. But it explained why Frankie wasn't too keen on chatting about what might be wrong with Tom. Stuff to do with hospitals must freak her out!

Regan quickly changed tack. 'Yeah, I bet you're right,' she said, trying hard to sound totally upbeat about it. 'Tom's gonna be just fine. So, what's the deal, huh? You want we should meet in the hospital, or what?'

'Yes, that'll be good,' said Frankie. 'I'll see you in the main entrance foyer, yeah? At about twelve o'clock.'

'No *problemo*,' said Regan. 'You bring the grapes, I'll make with the flowers.' An unpleasant thought slid into Regan's mind. 'Uh, Frankie, do you know if Rhea found out any more stuff about the . . . the bones?' A shiver ran down her back. 'Jeez – that was horrible to the max, wasn't it?'

'Tell me about it,' Frankie said with a shudder. 'I never want to see anything like that again. Never ever!' She pushed away the memory of the rolling and churning human bones. 'Jack didn't mention anything about it when he phoned,' she said. 'And to be honest, I'd rather not know. That is one dig I have absolutely no intention of ever going back to again. If all those poor people need putting back to rest, then Rhea can do it on her own.'

'No argument from me on that,' said Regan. 'And I guess you can take that with golden bells on as far as Tom is concerned! He had a lucky escape down there. He could have been . . . well . . . you know.'

'Yes.' Frankie knew. She knew exactly what Regan meant. Tom had been lucky to get away so lightly.

Very lucky.

CHAPTER FOUR
The Tolling Bell

Jack stood staring down at Tom's empty bed. Usually at this time on a Sunday morning, there would be a long Tom-shaped lump under the duvet. Or if he was up, Tom would be hurtling around the house creating bad smells with his chemistry set or causing chaos with his half-baked experiments in physics.

Only yesterday Jack had complained about having to share a room with Tom and his clutter. But right now Jack would have given anything to have Tom back there.

The Christmas family had only been in Lychford for a few months. There were enough rooms in their new home for Tom to have his own space, but some work needed to be done on Tom's room before it could be habitable – something to do with damp in the walls – and meanwhile Tom and Jack had to share a room. Which could be annoying. But the way things were, Jack wouldn't have minded sharing a shoebox with his younger brother if it meant Tom was back home again rather than lying in that hospital bed.

It was all very low-key, but Jack sensed that Dr Fairfax was concerned about the feverish symptoms that had followed Tom's accident with the filthy water. Jack hadn't mentioned it to anyone, but the incident last evening when Tom had seemed to believe he had the plague, had really shaken him. Certainly, Tom could simply be suffering from fevered dreams, but Jack was a little concerned that something else might be going on.

A kind of sixth sense existed in some members of the Christmas family. It flowed down the maternal line. Gran – their mum's mum – had it. And the boys' mother had it too: she could tell you what the weather was going to be like several days in advance, and she could find lost things just by thinking about them.

This strange legacy had manifested itself in Jack, too, although it was erratic and uncontrollable. He would sometimes sense things, like Dr Fairfax's concerns about Tom; but at other times, times when a sixth sense might be an advantage – like to warn Tom of the imminent collapse of that wall – it failed him completely.

The power – if that's what it was – had never shown itself in Tom. Jack had been glad of that, for Tom's sake. The strange family ability was more of a burden than a gift. Jack explained it to his curious younger brother in this way:

'Imagine you were born blind, but that every now and then, for no reason, you just got a flash of sight. And then everything went dark again with no explanation. Imagine how frustrating that would be:

to see for just a few seconds. Not for long enough to enjoy it or make use of it, but for just long enough to know what you're missing. It's worse than never seeing at all. Much worse.'

Jack almost resented this unwelcome gift, and the only people outside his immediate family who even knew about it were Frankie and Regan – and they were sworn to secrecy. But now Jack had the uneasy suspicion that Tom was showing signs of the awakening of the family power. Tom's half-memory of a huge black bird and his talk of a mass grave full of plague victims both sounded unsettlingly like the sort of garbled glimpses that Jack himself sometimes had of the shadowy, uncanny world of the sixth sense.

Jack hoped it was only feverishness. That haywire, unfathomable power was not something he'd wish on his worst enemy.

Jack turned from his silent contemplation of Tom's neatly made bed and stared out of the window down into their rough-and-ready back garden. Their mother was right at the far end, digging a patch of wasteland. A vegetable patch in the spring if the soil had any life in it. The work didn't need to be done for months yet. She said it gave her something to concentrate on. Something to fill her mind while they waited for the results of Tom's tests.

A grand old oak tree stood, gnarled and ancient, at the top end of the lawn. Birds played among the branches. Flashes of blue and green and white.

An image bled into Jack's consciousness. Rhea Peake. Walking up their front path.

The doorbell rang. Jack's dad was out working. He was a landscape gardener and he had an important client to see that morning. A big new contract, with any luck. He had the mobile with him in case anything happened. 'Not that it will,' their mother had said. Wishful thinking or sixth sense? Jack didn't know.

The bell was inaudible from the end of the garden. Jack went to answer the door.

'Hi there, Jack.' Rhea looked tired and drawn. She was wearing dark glasses. 'Sorry to bother you on a Sunday morning.'

'No problem,' said Jack. He stood aside as an invitation for her to enter the house. She hesitated on the step.

'I don't think I'll come in, thanks,' she said. 'I just wanted to know how Tom was getting along.' Her face was wrung with distress. 'It was all my fault.'

'You weren't to know what would happen,' said Jack. 'It was Tom who kicked the wall.'

'Yeah, but I shouldn't have let you people down there until all the health and safety checks had been done on the site. There are regulations, you see, and I . . . well, I more or less broke every rule in the book.'

'It was still an accident,' said Jack. 'Anyway, Tom will be OK.' He gave her a reassuring smile. 'And maybe it'll teach him not to lose his temper next time.'

Rhea reflected a weak smile back at him. 'Professor Paulson has suspended me from the team,' she said. 'I've just been speaking to him. I'm not his favourite person right now. And I've still got to tell my parents. They're not going to be too impressed, I can tell you. They're funding me and paying for my flat while I'm working on Professor Paulson's

31

team. Dad will have a fit. He bought me a car and everything, so I could . . . well . . .' She looked guiltily at him. Like a scolded spaniel. 'You don't want to hear my problems.'

Jack made a noncommittal sound in his throat. He didn't want to be unsympathetic – Rhea was clearly devastated by the accident – but on the other hand, if she hadn't said it would be all right for them to go and see the site, Tom's mishap would never have happened.

'Anyway,' said Rhea. 'Enough about me. How is Tom?'

'They kept him in,' said Jack. 'They're doing tests. We should hear the results this afternoon.'

Rhea's forehead contracted into a sea of wrinkles. 'Could you tell me which ward he's in? I'd like to go and visit him.'

'I'm not sure that's such a good idea,' said Jack. He had the feeling that Rhea was the last person Tom would want to see right then.

'I'd really like to,' Rhea said. 'It would mean a lot to me if I could just tell him how sorry I am about what happened.'

Jack hesitated. Rhea seemed very anxious to try and make amends. 'I suppose it'd be OK, if you really want to,' he said. 'But I think I'd better come along with you.' A faint smile lifted the corner of his mouth. 'Just in case he feels like beating you up.'

'There's no need,' said Rhea. 'I don't want to put you out. I'll be fine on my own.'

Jack frowned. 'You wouldn't be putting me out,' he said. 'He's my brother. I was going later anyway.'

'Yes. Of course. Sorry.' Rhea chewed her bottom lip. 'What do they think is wrong with him?'

Jack shook his head. 'Nothing, probably. They're just being thorough. He was feeling a bit sick and woozy last night. Hardly surprising in the circumstances. All that grotty water.' He looked at Rhea. 'Did Professor Paulson say anything about the . . . you know . . . the bones?'

Rhea nodded miserably. 'Yes. I was right – sort of. God, I feel such an idiot, Jack! Remember I told you Professor Paulson was doing some research on the area – to try and find out what might have been on that site between the thirteenth and nineteenth centuries?'

'Yes. I remember.' A shiver of concern snaked up Jack's spine. Rhea was about to say something that he would find very alarming. But what?

'He found out,' Rhea said dully. 'It's not very nice, I'm afraid. It's hard to see how the records got lost or mislaid or forgotten or whatever happened, but it seems . . .' Rhea took a long, slow deep breath. 'But it seems that the land adjacent to where we uncovered the remains of the tannery was used in the seventeenth century as a mass grave for victims of bubonic plague.'

Jack felt as if he'd been punched in the stomach.

Rhea looked anxiously at him. 'It was dug in the summer of 1665, according to the records Professor Paulson found. Those skeletons were . . . They died . . .' She swallowed hard. 'It was a plague pit, Jack.'

Frankie freewheeled her bike down the long sloping road that would ultimately take her to the hospital. Her golden hair floated in the cooling wind of her accelerating speed. The sensation of cold air on

33

her face was lovely, especially after two weeks of stifling heat. Tall and lively and athletic, Frankie loved to feel the sun on her skin, but this year the summer was behaving very badly. There hadn't been a breeze for a long time to stir the torpid air that filled the sweltering streets of Lychford. Summer lolled over the small town like a drunken man, too stupid with alcohol to move his smothering weight.

The wheels of the bike skimmed the road. There was no other traffic. Frankie half-closed her bright, sea-grey eyes. The long, wind-smacked descent of Lawrence Hill was as refreshing as a plunge into cold water.

She eased on the brakes as she neared the bottom of the hill. Roads fed off a roundabout. The town centre lay straight ahead. The road to the right would take you to London. To the left lay St Jude's church and, half a mile further on, where the town hemmed the countryside, was the hospital.

Frankie took the narrow road that passed the church. Tall trees, clad in midsummer green, lined the road, throwing down dappled shade. The solemn sound of a solitary bell vibrated in the air.

Doom!

Frankie had lived in Lychford all her life. She knew the bright, cascading trill of the bells of St Jude's church, but she had never before heard that single, deep, muffled tone.

Doom!

Its mournful toll hung heavy in the air.

Frankie brought her bike to a standstill.

Doom!

The morning service would surely be over by now

34

– so what was the reason for that lonely bell to be rung? And why did it sound so unbearably doleful?

Doom!

Frankie propped her bike against a tree and walked towards the lich-gate of the old church. The sixteenth-century building had been cleaned recently and the white stone of its great soaring tower shone in the sun. Light flared on the tall stained-glass windows.

Doom!

The air reverberated with the sounding of the bell. But the note was deadened, as though the bell was swathed in felt.

She walked in under the covered lich-gate. Frankie knew about lich-gates: many churches still had them. In olden days these roofed gates would be used during funerals as a temporary resting place for the bier. *Lich* came from the Old English word *lic*, meaning corpse.

Doom!

The air was cold under the slated roof.

She stepped through into the churchyard. The air was still strangely cool. Frankie looked up. A thin veil of cloud had covered the sun.

She walked up the brown gravel path, passing between neat lawns. A man was stooping by a leaning, lichen-green gravestone, trimming the errant grass with clacking shears. The most recent gravestone was dated 1864.

'Hello!' Frankie called.

The man straightened up, a hand in the small of his back. Frankie had seen him many times before. An elderly man who looked after the churchyard.

He wore a shapeless brown hat and his longish grey hair fell into his eyes.

He wiped his forehead. 'Hello, there,' he said. 'Hot work in this weather, eh?'

'Yes. I can see.' Frankie smiled. 'Can you tell me – what's the bell for? I've never heard it before.'

The elderly man blinked at her. 'What bell's that, m'dear?'

'The bell that—' Frankie stopped in mid-sentence. She twisted her head and looked up at the rearing white church tower. The bell had ceased tolling. 'Oh! It's stopped now!' she said. She looked at him. 'It was just ringing,' she said. 'It was going *bong*.' She left a long pause. '*Bong*.' Pause. '*Bong*. Just like that.' She pulled her hair off her face and flicked it over her shoulder. 'Was it for something special? It sounded very sad.'

'There's been no bell ringing here since before the service, m'dear,' said the old man. 'And that'd be more than an hour back.'

'Oh!' Frankie was astonished. Could the old man be deaf? Surely not. If he could hear her, then he'd definitely have been able to hear the melancholy bell.

'It'll be someone's television,' said the old man. 'Or a wireless. Kids have them blaring out of their cars these days like nobody's business. It's a wonder their brains don't turn to soup.' The old man grinned at the oddity of human behaviour. 'Sometimes all you can hear is the low notes. Throbbing away. Boom boom boom. They call it music. A load of screeching, I call it. No melody to speak of. It sounds like pigs mating. And I know what that sounds like, believe you me.'

36

'Um . . . yeah . . .' Frankie said vaguely. She probably had tapes back home, full of the sort of music he was describing. She loved heavy metal. She had her own electric guitar. But the sound she'd been hearing definitely wasn't bass-heavy rock music pumping out of someone's car.

Neither had it come from a loud television in a nearby house. She was sure of that. It hadn't been that sort of noise at all. Not a transmitted noise. It had been a real sound that had shivered the air all around her.

Doom!

A sorrowful, funereal sound that had tugged at her heart.

And yet the old man hadn't heard it.

How strange.

How very strange.

CHAPTER FIVE
The Emergence of Will Hilliard

Regan grinned as she scanned the buckets of cut flowers that filled one corner of the foyer of the hospital. She was going to present Tom with a bunch of flowers. Kill or cure: he'd either drop stone-dead of shock, or he'd be up out of that bed like a jack rabbit on springs.

A toothy, wedge-faced woman hovered while Regan made her choice.

'That one, please.'

The woman bombarded Regan with a smile. 'Lovely!'

'Yeah. I thought so.' A small posy of bright, cheerful flowers in a green wrap. Regan paid and pushed through the glass doors into the entrance hall. Signboards proliferated. Regan looked at the clock above the reception desk. It was ten past twelve.

There was no sign of Frankie. Maybe she'd already gone up?

Regan eyed the signposts. Complicated. She marched up to an important-looking man in a white coat and asked directions. Regan always took the most straightforward route out of a problem.

Five minutes later she found Tom's small side-room. There were four beds, but only one of them was occupied. Tom was lying on his back with his head turned to one side. His eyes were closed. Regan frowned. He looked very pale.

Frankie wasn't there. Regan considered tiptoeing away and waiting for Frankie down in reception. Maybe they should come back some other time.

She stepped lightly into the room, planning on leaving the flowers beside him on the bed. That'd fox him. An unknown admirer. Neat!

Tom's hazel eyes flickered open. He let out an audible breath.

'Jane!' his voice was a weak croak. 'Praise be! I thought you dead.'

Regan stopped in her tracks.

'*Jane?*' she said in surprise. 'Who the heck is *Jane?*'

Tom smiled fondly at her and reached out a hand as if he expected her to take it.

She gave a bark of laughter. 'You might be ill, man, but no way are we sitting here holding hands. Here, take these.' She pushed the bunch of flowers into his hand. But his fingers didn't grip. The wrap fell to the floor. Tom was still gazing at her in that weird, over-friendly way. Like he was soft on her or something.

'Well, thanks, Tom,' Regan said, squatting to pick the flowers up. 'Glad you liked 'em.'

Tom leaned awkwardly towards her over the bed and his hot, damp hand pressed against her cheek.

'I dreamed you had all died,' he said. 'You, and

Molly and Hugh and Nicholas. All dead.' His eyes were glassy.

Regan peeled his sweaty hand off her face. 'Uh, that's just fine, Tom. You're . . . looking, uh, you're looking good. How are they treating you?'

'Mama and Papa?' Tom asked in that same intense, reedy whisper. 'Do they live also? Are all the bad things not true, Jane? I have suffered such dreams. Have I had the sickness long?'

Regan stared into his face. He wasn't kidding her. Boy! Frankie hadn't warned her that he was this out of it. The poor guy was delirious to the max.

But it was kind of intriguing, all the same. Just exactly what was going on in Tom's head? And how come he was talking in that weird, old-fashioned way?

'Do you know who I am?' Regan asked gently.

Tom smiled weakly. 'Do not sport with me, Jane. I am too weary for your foolish devices.'

'I'm Jane, yeah?'

'No! You are Titania, Queen of the Faeries!' said Tom. He laughed, but it quickly changed to a feeble cough. 'I am so sick, Jane. What misery has come upon our family.' His eyes wandered around the room. 'I do not know this place.'

'You're in hospital, Tom.'

'Do that no more, I beg you.'

'Huh? Say *what?*'

'I do not like *Tom.* Use my proper name.' A bad light flared in his eyes. 'Are you an angel, Jane? Have you come to guide me from this place into paradise?'

Regan frowned. She gripped Tom's loose hand

40

and gave his fingers a hard wrench to one side. He grimaced and pulled his hand away.

'Does that feel like an angel?' she asked. 'Come on, Tom, pull yourself together. You're Tom Christmas and you're in hospital in Lychford, and you swallowed a whole lake of filthy water cos you were trying to—'

'I am Will Hilliard,' said Tom. 'And you are not my sister! You are some devil sent to torment me.' With a surprising burst of energy, he pushed Regan away. She bounced on her behind on the cold, hard floor.

'Hey! Quit that!'

Tom scrambled up and away from her, his face distorted with fear and horror.

'Avaunt, devil! I will have no commerce with you. I am a good Christian child.' His voice, still thin, had risen to a shrill wail. 'I see you now. I know you. They are all dead! All dead! Mama and Papa and Nicholas and Hugh and Molly and Jane. All dead. It was no dream. I dream now, and you are a demon sent to torment me on my deathbed!'

Regan clambered to her feet. 'Yeah, right!' She clamped her hands on her hips. 'Now you just snap out of this, Tom, or I'll have to call the guys with the white coats and the big butterfly nets. They'll cart you off, man! Listen – I'm Regan Vanderlinden and you're Tom Christmas, right? We drive each other crazy. You can't have forgotten *that*! Jeez, Tom, we're pals, man – stop this!' She stamped her foot. 'Stop this right *now*! You're weirding me out!'

All through this, Tom sat cocooned in bedcovers, staring at her with disturbed eyes. Trembling slightly.

Grey-faced. It was as if she was talking gibberish. Nothing she said seemed to register with him.

'Regan? What's going on?' The sudden voice behind her almost rocketed Regan clear through the ceiling. She spun on her heel. Jack and Rhea stood in the doorway. Jack was staring past her, his anxious eyes fixed on Tom.

'Jack! Thank heavens!' Regan gasped. 'Tom's gone completely . . . uh . . . he's . . . I . . . I can't get any sense out of him, Jack. It's like he's in another world. Truly! He thinks I'm an evil demon or something!'

Jack and Rhea goggled at her.

'Tom?' Jack moved into the room. 'Are you OK?'

'Oh, hello, Jack,' said Tom. 'I feel dead woozy.' He slid bonelessly down onto the bed and dragged the covers up over him. 'It's really cold in here. Where's Mum? Did you bring any mags?'

Regan turned slowly and gazed at him.

Tom blinked at her. 'What are *you* staring at?' he said.

'I don't know,' Regan said quietly. 'What *am* I staring at?'

Tom looked at his brother. 'Has she gone potty, or something?'

'Me?' Regan exploded. 'Have I gone potty? Oh, that's just great, Tom! I've just had to deal with the most bizarre conversation of my entire life, and you've got the nerve to ask if *I'm* crazy! It ain't me who's crazy, buster!'

'Regan,' Jack said. 'Don't yell at him.'

'I'm not yelling,' Regan yelled.

'I think you'll find you are,' Jack said mildly.

Regan closed her eyes and took a deep breath.

She smoothed the air around her with spread-fingered hands on stiff arms. 'Calm,' she said. 'Total calm.' She opened her eyes and fixed a stony glare onto Tom. 'Was that some kinda dumb joke just now?'

'What are you talking about?' asked Tom.

'You really don't remember?' Regan asked suspiciously.

Tom looked at his brother. 'What's she talking about?' he asked. 'I'm not up to this kind of thing. I feel rotten.'

Regan looked at Jack. She was baffled.

Rhea stood in the doorway, temporarily forgotten – watching Tom intently from behind her dark glasses.

'He was different a minute back,' Regan said. 'He was talking real funny, and he was coming out with a whole bunch of—'

'Later, Regan,' Jack interrupted her. 'Don't worry about it. You probably disturbed him in the middle of a dream.'

'Whoo!' breathed Regan. 'Some dream!'

Rhea stepped forwards into the room and stood at the foot of the bed. Tom looked at her without speaking. She licked her lips nervously.

'How are you?' she asked.

'Fine.' There was no expression in his voice.

A pained grimace tweaked at her face.

'Hardly that,' she said. 'I can't tell you how sorry I am about all this. I'd rather have had the wall fall on me than for you to be hurt.'

'I'll go along with that,' said Tom.

There was an awkward silence.

'Tom, she's only trying to say sorry,' said Jack.

'Yeah,' added Regan. 'Who kicked the darned wall in the first place?'

Rhea shook her head. 'I can't turn the clock back, Tom,' she said. 'I would if I could. Truly. If there's anything I can do . . .?' Her voice trailed off.

Jack watched his brother closely. He seemed more or less like his old self. Certainly, he didn't look well enough to leap out of bed and race around the room, but the manic light had gone out of his eyes. He didn't seem so haunted as he had yesterday when they had been alone. But was he really getting better?

'Someone could have thought to bring me some grapes,' said Tom.

Jack smiled. Regan laughed.

'Frankie's doing that,' she said. 'If she ever gets here.' She bent down and scooped the flowers up off the floor. 'There y'go, dude,' she said in a silly, nasal voice. 'I brung ya some posies to cheer yez up.' She was about to push them at him when the waft of an entirely unexpected scent hit her nostrils.

She gingerly lifted the flowers to her nose and gave a cautious sniff.

'Aw, Jeez!' she groaned. 'I don't believe it!'

Rising from the colourful congregation of flowers was the distinct smell of vinegar.

CHAPTER SIX
Crazy Tom

Regan shoved the reeking flowers into Jack's face.

'Regan!' he exclaimed, jerking his head back. 'Watch it!'

'Smell 'em!' she demanded.

Jack sniffed. He shrugged. 'Flowers. So what?'

'What do they smell of?' asked Regan.

'Sorry?'

'Smell!' Regan said. 'Smell 'em properly! What do they smell of to you?'

Jack sniffed again. 'They smell of flowers,' he said.

Regan tried the same technique with Rhea. She got the same answer.

She stared at the innocent flowers with hooded eyes. 'Ohh . . . kayyy . . .' she said. 'So . . . my nose has gone insane.'

'Why? What do they smell like to you?'

'Vinegar!'

From the bed, Tom let out a splutter of laughter.

'I've been smelling vinegar all morning,' Regan explained. 'It must just be me.' She dropped the flowers onto Tom's stomach. 'Get well soon,' she said. 'Hope you enjoy them.'

'Thanks,' said Tom, eyeing the flowers as if Regan had just landed him with a poisonous snake. 'Er . . . what do I do with them?'

Rhea smiled. 'Put them in water,' she said. 'Maybe someone could go and find a vase?'

'I'm on it,' said Regan. She marched out.

Rhea moved to the side of the bed. She picked up the flowers and began to peel off the tape that held the wrapping paper.

'I meant what I said,' she told Tom. 'If there's anything I can do to help.' She unwound the paper from the flower stems and laid them on the bedside table. 'Would you like something to drink?' she said suddenly. She pulled a bottle of dark fizzy drink out of her jacket pocket.

Tom smiled. 'Yes. Thanks. All they've been giving me is water.' He looked at the label. 'Cherry cola,' he said. 'Great!'

A cold feeling invaded Jack's chest, like a dead hand pressing over his heart.

'I don't think you should drink that,' he said as Tom twisted the bottle's cap.

'Why not?'

'I don't think you should eat or drink anything without asking first,' said Jack. 'Just in case.'

'In case of what?' Tom frowned at the bottle. 'Hey, the cap didn't go schputt like they're supposed to when you open them.' The bottle was capped by one of those tamper-proof lids that are put on under pressure. There had been no pop when Tom had screwed it off. He looked at Rhea. 'You should go back to the place where you bought it and complain,' he said. 'Someone's been at it.'

'I shouldn't think so,' said Rhea. 'It'll be OK, I'm sure. Drink it.'

Tom shook his head and put the bottle on the bedside table. 'Thanks, but I'd rather not. What if the shopkeeper's had a slurp out of it? Yuck!'

Jack sat on the edge of Tom's bed. 'Do you remember the chat we had yesterday about what came out through the wall when it fell in?' he asked.

'Yeah, of course,' Tom said. 'The bones.' His forehead contracted into wrinkles. 'At least . . . I . . .' He looked at Jack. 'No, I don't remember it at all. Isn't that weird? I know you told me something, but I can't remember what.'

'You were tired, I expect,' said Jack. 'Anyway, Rhea's found out all about it.' He looked up at the young woman. She was staring at Tom, or seemed to be – it was hard to tell with her eyes hidden behind those shades. Her mouth was a tight line. 'Haven't you, Rhea?'

She came out of some private thoughts. 'Yes,' she said. 'It's not very nice, Tom. The remains came from a plague pit.'

Tom closed his eyes. His face was ash-grey against the white of the pillowslip.

'Great,' he said softly.

Rhea chewed her bottom lip. 'I've spoken to Professor Paulson,' she said. 'The site's been sealed off now. He says you can't . . . er . . . I mean, it's not like you could catch anything . . . er . . .' She glanced at Jack. ' . . . From the remains, I mean. It's not . . . um . . . infectious or contagious or whatever the

47

word is. There's nothing like that to worry about. It's just . . . just . . .'

'Just horrible,' whispered Tom, his eyes still closed.

'A-actually,' stammered Rhea, 'the 1660s – when the plague hit Lychford worst – is a really i-interesting time . . . for . . . er, for people who are into archaeology and history. You know?'

Tom stared at her. 'Interesting?' he said softly. He closed his eyes and turned his head away from her. 'Un-be-lievable!'

'Sorry,' muttered Rhea. 'I think maybe I'd better be going.' She turned her hidden eyes to Jack. 'Sorry.'

She made as if to touch Tom's shoulder, but drew her hand back before making contact.

'Could I come and see you again some time?' she asked.

Tom grunted.

She picked up the bottle of cherry cola and thrust it into her pocket.

'I'll be off then.'

'Bye,' said Tom.

With lowered head, Rhea left.

'That wasn't very kind,' said Jack, batting Tom's arm with the back of his hand. 'She was feeling bad enough without you being nasty to her.'

'She deserves it,' said Tom. 'Fancy telling me that having a load of plaguey bodies fall all over me is supposed to be *interesting*!'

'That's not exactly what she said,' Jack pointed out. 'And they weren't actual bodies.' Tom opened his mouth to protest. 'Yeah, yeah, I know,' Jack said. 'It was still a complete nightmare down there. It was no picnic for the rest of us, Tom. Trust me. But Rhea was right, in a way. I bet it is an interesting period to look into.'

'Yeah, well, feel free!' Tom declared. 'I'll just lie here and carry on being ill, if that's OK with you.'

Jack gave him a long, slow look. 'How *do* you feel?' he asked. 'You seem better . . . a bit.'

'I feel like a total wooze-box,' said Tom. 'I keep getting dizzy and losing track of what I'm doing.' He paused. 'What was Regan talking about just now? She said I was acting funny. I don't remember it.'

'I don't know,' said Jack. 'I wasn't here. But you were behaving strangely yesterday. You said something really, really peculiar. I told you that Rhea thought the bones came from an abandoned graveyard, and you said – no, they were from a mass grave . . . of people who had the plague.'

'I never!'

'You did.'

Tom stared at him. '*You* must have said something about it.'

'Nope. I only found out about it this morning. But you knew last night.'

'Ohhhh.'

There was a long silence between the two brothers.

'Jack?' Tom asked reluctantly, not wanting to hear the answer he thought his brother might give. 'How could I have known that?'

Jack stared out of the window. 'You tell me,' he sighed.

'Yo! Frankie! You're late, man. Where've you been?' Regan was heading back to Tom's room with a vase

49

of water in her fist when the lift doors opened further along the corridor and Frankie stepped out.

'It took longer to get here than I expected,' said Frankie. She'd decided the bell must have been in her head all along. Brain playing tricks. She looked at the vase. 'Invisible flowers. Nice.'

Regan grinned. 'Yeah, I got them from the invisible flower seller outside. Did you see her?'

'No. The one I saw was completely visible,' said Frankie. 'I got these.' She held open a paper bag. Grapes.

Regan dipped in, tugged a couple off the vine and threw them into her mouth.

'How's the patient?' Frankie asked.

'Don't ask!' Regan said vehemently. 'I mean it, Frankie. Just don't ask me how that guy is. I've just had the weirdest ten minutes of my entire life with him.' Her eyebrows knitted. 'These grapes smell—' Her mouth shut like a steel box.

'What?'

'Nothing. C'mon, let's see how Crazy Tom the Mudhopper is getting along.'

They found Tom and Jack sitting in silence in the clean little side room.

'Surprise!' Frankie sang, waving the bag of grapes. 'Party time.' The two boys looked dully at her. The bag drooped in her hand. 'Oh. Maybe not, then.'

'Rhea gone?' asked Regan.

Jack nodded.

'Did you two know it was a plague pit that fell in on me?' asked Tom.

The expressions on the girls' faces said it all.

'A . . . plague . . . pit . . .?' said Frankie. 'As in the Great Plague?'

'Apparently,' said Tom.

'Wow,' Regan breathed. 'Like, with the black rats and the fleas and the biting and the dropping dead and all that? Urrgh, that's so yucky! No wonder you're freaking out, Tom!'

'Who's freaking out?' Tom said affrontedly.

'Not ten minutes ago,' said Regan, 'in this very room, you told me you were Will Hilliard and that all your family were dead. Heck, man, you thought I was a demon of some sort.'

'That last bit sounds about right,' said Tom. 'But if all that really happened – how come I don't remember it?' He looked at his brother. 'You remember the strange stuff that happens in your head, don't you?'

'Yes,' Jack said quietly. 'I don't always understand it, but I do remember it.'

'Do you think Tom is getting your second sight thing?' asked Regan. 'Cool!'

'It's not second sight,' snapped Jack. Discussing his strange gift always made him uncomfortable.

'Whatever!' Regan said, unperturbed. 'Is that what's making Tom act crazy? Crazier than normal, I mean.'

'I don't know,' said Jack. 'I suppose it might be.'

Tom leaned back into the pillows. 'I wish you'd all go away and leave me alone,' he said. 'My head hurts.' His eyes closed tiredly. His reserves of strength were just about gone.

'Do you want to sleep?' asked Frankie.

Tom's eyes opened. 'It was different,' he said. 'This place. It was different before. Darker. Smellier. And there was a big bird . . .' His eyes stared into the distance as the memory leaked back into his throbbing head. 'A big black bird.'

'You mentioned that before,' said Jack. 'Where do you think you were, Tom?'

'Here,' Tom said firmly. 'I was right here, but this place was totally different. It was horrible. People were dying all over the place. I could hear them coughing and making groaning noises all around me. Then the big black bird came.' He stared at Jack. 'If this is what your special powers do, then I don't want them!' He grabbed convulsively at his brother's wrist. 'Get rid of them, Jack – please. Get rid of them for me! I don't want to be like this.'

Voices in the corridor. All eyes turned to the door. Mrs Christmas appeared, accompanied by Dr Fairfax. Both smiled at Tom in a way that Jack didn't find entirely comforting. It was a look-on-the-bright-side sort of smile.

'Hello,' Mrs Christmas said, 'it looks like we've got a room full.' She looked across at Tom. 'I hope they're not tiring you out, Tom.' Regan and Frankie got out of the way. Mrs Christmas went over and kissed Tom on the forehead. 'How are you feeling?'

'A bit yucky. Can I go home?'

'Soon,' said the doctor.

'How soon?' asked Jack.

'As soon as possible,' said the doctor with a smile. 'We don't like people cluttering up our beds for no good reason. But we have to make just a couple more tests.'

'Have you had the results of the tests you've already carried out?' asked Jack.

'Dr Fairfax says they're not as conclusive as he'd have liked,' Mrs Christmas said, stroking Tom's lank brown hair. 'He thinks you've got some kind of mild infection from the water you swallowed.' She smiled reassuringly. 'All he needs to do is track down exactly what germs are in there, then he'll know how to treat them and get you better.'

'It shouldn't take more than a couple of days, tops,' said the doctor.

'But I feel fine,' protested Tom.

'I doubt that very much,' said Dr Fairfax. 'I've spoken on the phone with Professor Paulson. He's filled me in on all the details of the mess you fell into.'

'Actually, the mess fell on me,' Tom said softly.

The doctor smiled. 'Listen, Tom. At best you've swallowed a lot of filthy water. And according to what Professor Paulson told me about the conditions down in that cellar, you could easily have ingested some nasty germs at the same time. That's why we need to keep a close eye on you.'

Tom felt too drained to argue. The past few hours had been exhausting and debilitating. At first he had been throwing up all the time, and when he went to the toilet it was thin and watery and horrible. He ached all over, and there was a constant pain in his head: like an iron band tightening around his skull.

'I want to monitor your temperature,' said Dr Fairfax. 'And your blood pressure is a little bit low, so I need to watch that. And we have to make sure that you aren't becoming dehydrated. That could cause very serious problems.'

Tom looked at him with anxious eyes.

'That won't happen if you stay here and rest,' said Dr Fairfax. 'You're going to be just fine, Tom. That's a promise.'

The doctor rounded the bed and sat at Tom's side. Tom was asked to sit up and open his pyjama jacket. Everyone could see how much effort it took for Tom to lift himself up off the pillows. His meagre store of energy had been drained by the events of the afternoon. Despite what he said, Tom felt – and looked – weak as a stranded fish. The illness – whatever it was – had a good hold on him.

Dr Fairfax pressed a stethoscope to Tom's chest. 'Deep, slow breaths, please, Tom.'

The check only took a couple of minutes. Tom was relieved to be allowed to flop back. He felt like he'd just run up a mountain with lead weights tied to his back. Strength seemed to be pouring out of him like water out of a cloth bag.

'Are you drinking?' asked the doctor. 'You should drink plenty of water. It will help replace all the fluid you've lost.' There was a jug of water by the bed, and a glass.

The doctor looked around at everyone. 'I think it might be wise to give him a chance to sleep now.' He poured water into the glass. 'Mum can stay, but it's probably best for the rest of you to go pretty soon.'

He handed the glass to Tom. 'There you go,' he said gently. 'Let me see you drink that.'

Tom's eyes flashed. 'Get away from me!' His voice was a shrill whirl of anger and fear. He lashed out, knocking the glass out of the doctor's hand. 'I won't drink it! I won't!'

The glass rolled off the bed, spilling water. It smashed on the floor.

'Tom!' cried his mother.

The doctor tried to restrain Tom, but he struggled

and fought, his face twisted in panic. He jerked an arm free and sent the water jug spinning.

Smash! Regan jumped back as a spray of water and glass fragments splashed up close to her legs.

'Tom! For heaven's sake, calm down!' said the doctor. He held Tom by the shoulders, rising to bear Tom down onto the bed, to still his violent thrashing.

The room was stunned.

And then, as suddenly as it had come, Tom's furious outburst ebbed away and his straining body became limp under the doctor's hands.

'I'm ... sorry ...' he gasped, his eyes swimming. 'I'm ... sorry ...'

CHAPTER SEVEN
Pestilence

'What the heck do you think all that was about?' asked Regan. 'He flipped, didn't he? Like, totally!'

The three friends were outside the hospital, Jack and Regan waiting while Frankie unchained her bike. Tom had fallen into a fretful sleep only seconds after his outburst. His mother was staying with him, but the others had left. Jack half-wanted to stay, but he needed to talk privately with his friends.

Frankie looked anxiously at Jack. He was staring into the distance, his wide-spaced brown eyes vague and unfocused. 'What do you think's wrong with him?' she asked. Jack didn't answer.

'I don't get it,' said Regan. 'One minute he's pretty much normal, then he's off in Neverland.'

'That's what happens with fever, isn't it?' said Frankie. 'Hallucinations and stuff. Has he got some kind of fever, do you think?'

'Fever doesn't help you know things you can't possibly know,' said Jack. He looked at the two girls. 'Tom knew the bones were from a plague pit before anyone else did.' He looked at Regan. 'What exactly happened before we got there?'

As best she could, Regan described the aberrant conversation she'd had with Tom – or, rather, with the person who called himself Will Hilliard.

'And then when you and Rhea arrived,' she finished, 'it was like he threw a switch and came back into the real world again.'

'Did he say what the other people died of?' asked Jack.

'No, but by the way he was talking, it was all pretty nasty. He thought his whole family had died and that he was next on the list.'

'And he told me that he imagined he'd been in some place where people were coughing and moaning,' said Jack. 'A horrible place where people were dying all around him.'

'You think he's having some kind of flashbacks, don't you?' Frankie said to Jack. 'You don't think this is just a fever – you think something else is going on.'

'I don't know what I think,' said Jack. 'But I wish there was some way of finding out if there ever was a person called Will Hilliard.'

'And when he lived,' said Regan.

'And whether he died of the plague,' Frankie murmured.

'Oh, wow!' breathed Regan. 'Could he be, like, *possessed* by the ghost of some guy who died of plague back in the seventeenth century? Is that possible?'

They looked at one another. A couple of months ago they would have laughed at the idea, but they had all experienced things in the recent past which made them far less sceptical of the supernatural.

Strange things lurked in the shadows cast by even the most innocent of summer suns. Sometimes these things reached out into the real world. Then there was trouble.

Jack took a deep breath. 'I think we need to know a lot more about what we're dealing with here,' he said. 'I don't know if Tom's possessed – or even if that kind of thing can really happen, but if it can and he is, then we need to know a lot more about how things were around here in the middle of the seventeenth century. Because that's where all this stuff seems to be coming from.'

'Darryl!' said Frankie. 'He'll be able to help, I bet.'

Regan nodded. 'Yeah,' she said astutely. 'And he's the one guy around here who won't have us all shipped off to the funny farm the moment we open our mouths.'

It was agreed. They would go and pay a visit on Darryl Pepper. Frankie re-chained her bike. She'd pick it up later.

They headed for the bus stop.

Darryl Pepper lived a solitary, almost hermit-like existence in a huge junk-shop of a room crammed in under the roof of a dilapidated old Victorian house. The room was like an Aladdin's cave of bric-a-brac and disorder: old pieces of furniture in mid-repair, strange contraptions of wires and spindles and levers, half-constructed models, heaps of magazines and newspapers and books, parts of dusty motors and other unrecognizable machines, all fighting for space in there.

And amid all this chaos sat Darryl himself, thin

and angular as a stork, dressed in a terrible old green cardigan with a narrow tie at his long, scrawny neck. His short, pale hair stood up in spikes all over his head – crying out for a comb. His sharp eyes skidded around behind thick, horn-rimmed glasses. He had an Adam's apple the size of a golf ball. Darryl Pepper was only nineteen years old.

He sat in a small alcove, bathed in sunlight and working at his computer. The walls that hemmed him in were plastered with scraps and notes and shreds of paper that all meant something to him, if to no one else.

Not that anyone else ever came into that curious eyrie – not even the mad pixie of a landlady who inhabited a couple of rooms somewhere down in the back of the house – no one, that is, except for the four ACE members who had become Darryl's firm friends.

'So, you think something's come out of that pit and overrun Tom in some way,' Darryl asked. 'Is that it?' He was perched on the edge of his revolving chair, his neck stretched forwards and his hands clasped between his bony knees. Jack, Frankie and Regan were sitting on the dusty old cushions that Darryl had dug out especially for them.

'That just about covers it,' said Jack. 'It could all be nonsense, of course.'

'Absolutely,' said Darryl.

'Do *you* think it is?' Frankie asked him.

'Me?' Darryl smiled and his bright eyes flashed behind his spectacles. 'I don't know one way or another. But I think you're wise to do some research. If you want my advice, I think you should find out all you can about the plague itself, and how it would

59

have affected a town like Lychford. You might even turn up some information about the Hilliards – that was the name, wasn't it?'

'Will Hilliard,' said Regan. 'That's right.' She looked thoughtful. 'But what's there to know about the plague? It was caused by rats and it was wiped out by the Great Fire of London. End of story.'

Darryl smiled. 'Entirely wrong,' he said.

'Huh?'

'The Great Plague of London was just a particularly violent outbreak of a disease that had been ravaging Europe on and off for centuries,' said Darryl. 'It's a fascinating story, actually. It was certainly around in Roman times, and it's even thought to have contributed to the collapse of their Empire. Way back in the fourteenth century, there were tales of terrible disasters that were ripping through China.' Darryl took off his glasses and polished them on his tie, his eyes misty as he continued to speak. 'Of course, you have to appreciate that in the fourteenth century, China was . . .' he shrugged, 'a bizarre place, so far away that for most people the distances involved didn't make any kind of sense.'

'Most people didn't even move out of their own village in those days, did they?' said Jack.

'Absolutely,' said Darryl. He replaced his glasses on his long, pointed nose. 'Terrible stories came down the trade routes from Cathay – that's what they called China in those days. Traders told of droughts and famines and floods and earthquakes.' He grinned wolfishly. 'There was sickness and pestilence. Plagues of locusts. You know, all that kind of miserable stuff. And, of course the actual plague itself. But it was all pretty academic, until the plague hit the European ports.'

'Yeah, that's right,' said Frankie. 'I remember! It came with rats on ships.'

'Yes, we know that *now*,' said Darryl. 'But you've got to appreciate that no one had the foggiest idea what was going on at the time. They didn't even know that microbes and bacteria existed. Their best guess was that it was some kind of contamination of the air. They called it "the foul blast of wind out of the south".'

'Pretty dumb, huh?' said Regan.

'Not at all,' said Darryl. 'They were trying their best to make sense of something that was way out of their experience. One explanation – my favourite, actually – was that the disease had been caused because of a war between the sea and the sun out in the Indian Ocean. They reckoned that huge amounts of water had been sucked up during this war and that it just hung around in the air as a foul vapour – like a kind of horrible, contaminated mist – full of dead and rotting bits of fish. And they reckoned this mist drifted around, giving the plague to everyone it touched. They called it a miasma; a cloud of poison gas wandering about the world killing people left, right and centre.'

'I guess that made as much sense as anything else,' Regan admitted. 'It's kind of difficult to imagine how they figured stuff out in those days.'

'Oh, they had plenty of theories,' said Darryl. 'Some people said it was all due to the movements of the planets. Others thought it was a punishment from God. And there was even a theory that it was poisonous fumes from the centre of the earth, let out during earthquakes.'

'And it was the rats all along,' said Frankie. 'Hoo, boy!'

'Fleas carried by rats, at any rate,' said Darryl. 'But if you want to get an idea of what people thought at the time of the Great Plague, you should find yourselves a copy of Samuel Pepys's diaries. He was in London when it broke out.'

'Hey!' Frankie sat up. '*The Diary of Samuel Pepys*! I've heard of that. In fact, I think we've got a copy at home.'

'You should read it,' said Darryl. 'But if you people want some proper hard info on how the plague affected Lychford, there are a few local history books in the library.' He grinned and made a flicking gesture of his head towards the computer. It was on screensaver mode. Stars swarmed endlessly forwards. 'Not to mention the possibility of digging stuff up on the good old Internet.'

'Let's do that, then,' said Jack. 'Mum said they were doing some kind of stock-taking at the library today, so there'll be people there. They'll know me – they're bound to let me in.' Jack's mother was head librarian – it was this promotion which had brought the Christmas family to Lychford in the first place. 'So long as I keep out of everyone's way, I'm sure they won't mind me doing some quiet research in a corner. Anyone else interested?'

'If it's OK with Darryl,' said Regan, 'I'd rather stay here and take a look at the Internet.' She grinned at him. 'Wha'd'ya say, Darryl? Wanna surf the net with me?'

'That would be an interesting experience, I'm sure,' Darryl said, his eyes twinkling. 'Yes. Why not?'

'I'd better go and pick up my bike,' said Frankie. 'I don't want to leave it outside the hospital all day.' She looked at Jack. 'I'll probably come along and see how you're getting on a bit later.'

'OK,' said Regan. 'That's everyone fixed up.' She bounced off her cushion. 'Well?' she said, staring down at Jack and Frankie. 'Don't you folk have anywhere you need to be? Me and Darryl here have work to do.'

Darryl gave her an uneasy look. Yes, surfing the net with a live-wire like Regan was certainly going to be an interesting experience. He just hoped that he and his beloved computer would survive the onslaught.

CHAPTER EIGHT
The Great Plague of London

'**D**uring the Middle Ages, the word plague was used to cover all sorts of fatal epidemic diseases, but these days it is restricted to diseases caused by the bacillus *Yersinia pestis*.' Regan read the strange words slowly aloud. She grinned at Darryl. '*Pestis*, huh? As in pest, I guess.'

There was only the one chair in Darryl's computer alcove. Regan sat and Darryl leaned over her shoulder. They had found what they were looking for. Regan slid the computer mouse around on its mat. The pointer collided with another icon. Regan clicked and a new page scrolled down on the screen.

'The plague in humans has three forms.' Regan started reading aloud again. 'Bubonic plague is named after the large buboes: lumps caused by enflamed lymph nodes in the groin, armpit or neck.' She shuddered. 'The disease is transmitted by insects which live on rodents. The worst of these is the flea *Xenopsylla cheopis* which lives on black rats. In Pneumonic plague, the lungs are infected. This disease can be transmitted by coughs and sneezes. If the disease spreads into the bloodstream, it becomes Septicemic plague. This can also be caused by touch.' Regan leaned back. 'I always hated rats,' she said. 'It's just so totally incredible. One little flea-bite and you're out of here, just like that!' She snapped her fingers. 'Gone!'

'Click on the symptoms icon,' said Darryl. 'That's where it'll start getting really grisly.'

Regan tapped the mouse. A new page scrolled up.

'OK,' said Regan. 'What do we have here?' She read. 'The first symptoms of bubonic plague are headaches, nausea, vomiting, aching joints and a feeling of ill-health. Then the lymph nodes swell up and start to hurt. Temperature rises. Breathing becomes rapid. A raging brain-fever can produce the effects of insanity, causing the victim to laugh hysterically and become maniacal. In fatal cases, death occurs in about four days. In pneumonic plague, the victim coughs up blood – ew! Yuck!'

'Told you so,' said Darryl. Regan felt like she knew enough gruesome stuff by then, but Darryl carried on reading out loud from the screen. 'Death occurs in two to three days. In Septicemic plague the victim has a sudden high fever, turns dark purple within a couple of hours and will die the same day. The purple colour, which appears in the victims of all three types of plague, is caused by respiratory failure. This is why the disease was once known as the Black Death.'

'Cute name!' Regan said flatly. 'So their lungs just give up, yeah? Well, I'm really pleased about having all *that* information in my life! I can't wait to share it with the guys.' She looked around at Darryl. 'I'm sure glad it died out!'

Darryl didn't reply. He leaned over her and moved the mouse. Click. A new page scrolled up.

Regan read silently.

Her eyes opened wide. 'Ohhh!' The page held some disturbing information. She stared around at Darryl, her mouth half-open in shock. 'Is that true?'

Darryl nodded. 'I think it must be,' he said.

The last recorded outbreak of plague had occurred less than ten years ago.

Frankie settled down in the little-used spare bedroom in the back of the semi-detached house where she lived with her father and his new wife and their brand new baby.

Samantha, Frankie's new stepmother, was bearable – just about – but Frankie always had the feeling the woman didn't really like her. She'd heard Samantha complaining to her dad about her being 'precocious' – whatever that meant. And Samantha hated it when Frankie played her electric guitar up in her bedroom. She said it gave her migraine. Big shame! What about all the noise that baby Tabitha kicked up? Of course, that was different. And how did Samantha think Frankie felt when some total stranger came flouncing into the house trying to be her new mother!

Fortunately, baby Tabitha was a full-time obsession for Samantha, and so long as Frankie steered clear of them, arguments were kept down to a minimum. Frankie's best pal outside of the ACE gang was Katie March. She loved the idea of babies. She'd been quite stunned when Frankie had shown a total indifference to the squalling, wriggling infant. She thought Frankie was weird. Frankie liked weird.

The neglected spare bedroom had become a dumping-ground over the last twelve months: a rubbish tip for all the stuff that Samantha didn't like but which she couldn't persuade her husband Miles to throw out.

Among the piles of stuff Samantha didn't want were several cardboard boxes heaped higgledy-piggledy with books.

Frankie had last been in the room a couple of months back when a stone sculpture of a dolphin had disappeared mysteriously from the living room. She'd always liked that dolphin. Samantha had shoved it in the spare bedroom. Frankie had retrieved it, and now it was sitting on top of the guitar amplifier in her room. Out of bounds to Samantha.

It had been during the search for the discarded dolphin sculpture that Frankie had noticed the *Diary of Samuel Pepys*.

Frankie sat in a field of mid-afternoon sunlight on a pile of dusty old curtains in a far corner of the room. She opened the book. Inside was a scribbled dedication: *To Lizzie with love. Happy birthday. Mum and Dad*. Frankie gazed at the words. Lizzie was her mum's name. A tightness clenched in Frankie's chest and her eyes welled.

She scraped her sleeve across her eyes and pushed the sad feelings away. No good sitting there feeling sorry for herself. Things to do.

She started reading.

The patch of sunlight slid away from her as the afternoon progressed. It stretched itself out to the far wall and began to climb. It glinted on a framed picture of a ship with a square sail and a dragon figurehead. Something else Samantha hadn't liked. Idiot woman!

Every now and then, Frankie changed position on her makeshift cushion to ease numbed places and to stretch stiff parts. The diary was hard going – good old Samuel's style wasn't exactly user-friendly. But she persevered, skipping great dull chunks and searching out any reference to the plague. The diary went from January 1659 right through until 31st May 1669 – by which time the poor man was almost blind.

The first reference to the plague came fleetingly on June 16th 1664. *De Ruyter is dead, with fifty men of his own ship, of the plague, at Cales.* There was nothing more until September 23rd. *We were told today of a Dutch ship of 3 or 400 tons, where all the men were dead of the plague, and the ship cast ashore at Gottenburgh.*

After that, Pepys made no further comment on the disease until April 30th 1665, when he wrote of a great fear of the sickness in London and that several houses were already shut up and their people fled. The entry concluded *God preserve us all!*

And then it started. Entry after grim entry. Frankie read with absorbed horror as the catastrophe unfolded in those curious, dry old words of the long-dead diarist.

The doors of plague houses were cursed by a ragged cross of red paint, or by the words *Lord Have Mercy On Us All* scrawled red on the walls. By the end of June people were dying in their hundreds. A weekly Mortality Bill was produced.

Doom!

Soft as swan's down. Hardly to be heard. The sound of a distant bell.

Frankie looked up from the book. Disorientated. She was surprised to find herself at home. She had been so drawn into the diary that she'd almost felt like she was leaning over Samuel Pepys's bent shoulder as he wrote of the disaster that was over-whelming the helpless city.

July 13th – seven hundred died this week.

July 20th – one thousand eight hundred and nine dead this week.

July 27th – one thousand seven hundred dead.

London was in the grip of the plague.

Doom!

Frankie's eyes were jerked from the page again. Once could be imagination. Twice was real. Her heart pounded as she strained for a third dull summoning from the faraway bell. She realized she was gripping the book so tightly that her knuckles and her fingernails were white. She let out a pent-up gasp of breath. She willed her fingers to relax.

August 31st – six thousand one hundred and two died of the plague. But it is feared that the true number of the dead this week is near ten thousand.

September 7th – six thousand nine hundred and seventy-eight dead.

September 20th – seven thousand one hundred and sixty-five dead.

So many people dying.

Doom!

Frankie screamed and the book fell out of her hands. The bell tolled a long, shivering note, deep as dark water, mournful as despair. It was so close. As though the sound emanated from some dark, phantom bell-tower that threw its ghastly shadow over the very room in which she sat mortified.

Doom!

She was frozen. Like a fly in amber. Like a rabbit in headlights. Like a mouse under a cobra's stare. All she could do was wait. Wait and wait for the next dreadful peal from that dismal, resonant bell.

Doom!

It was calling her. The long, quivering note was ringing for her alone. Trembling, she stumbled to her feet. She walked to the window. With stiff fingers, she turned the latch. Thick, heavy air poured in as she forced the window open.

Doom!

The crazy-paved patio spread like a grey sheet, two floors below her. She climbed.

A shrill sound halted her. It swept through the dull webbing that had filled her head. The urgent, insistent squeal of a hungry or irritable baby. Tabitha.

She found herself with one knee up on the window sill, her hands gripping the frame, her other leg dangling.

She fell back into the room, her face running with cold sweat.

She knelt, doubled over, breathing fast. She dragged sticky hair off her cheeks. The book was face-up, open in front of her.

July 30th 1665 – It was a sad noise to hear our bells toll and ring so often today, either for deaths or burials; I think, five or six times.

With a jerk of her arm, Frankie flung the book closed. She scrambled to her feet and ran for the door. It slammed behind her as she made for the sanctuary of her own room.

She bolted her door from the inside and threw herself on the bed, dragging a pillow up over her head to cover her ears.

All she could hear in the stifling darkness was the wild throbbing of the blood through her veins.

The bell was silent.

CHAPTER NINE
A Bird of Ill Omen

The boy awoke out of darkness into pain and sickness and a weakness that made him feel like a thing made of damp and tattered paper. He didn't feel just desperately ill – he felt as though his body was coming apart. Falling all to pieces. Rags and shreds. Disintegrating.

A foul smell hung around him. Desperate animal noises crawled into his ears. Coughing. Groaning. Dying noises.

He opened his eyes. Light stabbed into his skull, dull but agonizing. A stained grey ceiling hung above him. There was a terrible, gnawing pain. He reached under the bedcovers and felt the hard, painful lumps. His fingers slid away.

Buboes.

Plague.

But another memory clung by its fingernails. A white room. Friendly faces. A clean smell. Confusion but much less pain. A vision. An angel come to lead him home.

Jane.

His sister Jane, come to take his hand and draw him up out of his sickbed. His dead sister Jane. Alive again. Her long black hair. Her broad, pale, clever forehead – full of thoughts. Her wide, friendly mouth.

But no. She was dead. They were all dead. He had seen Jane lying on her bed, her face a bruised purple mask, her limbs stiff. Her eyes open but empty.

The white room.

No. That was the dream. This was real.

He was in the pest house. The plague house. Mama and Papa and all the others were dead – and now he was dying. The last of the Hilliards.

He struggled in his weakness, throwing the thin blankets about as he writhed on the stinking bed. He lifted himself on an elbow. His head pounded. In the next bed a woman coughed. Red ran down her chin. Her face was dark and swollen.

But the boy had to speak. He had to tell someone the truth of what had happened in their house. He had to warn them about Dr Bludworth.

The boy let out a cry of despair. He fell back into dank sheets. Drained, floating on a sea of pain.

A great black bird emerged from the fog of his sickness. Its heavy black beak dipped, pointing at his heart. The bird stooped over him.

The boy tore at the dreadful beak. It broke away. He saw a face behind it. A human face.

He recognized it. Iron-grey hair. Skin like weathered stone. Malicious hooded eyes. The boy shrank from those eyes.

'Lord have mercy on us all.' A woman spoke from beyond the horizon of his sick-fogged vision.

Lord have mercy on us all.

*

It was mid-evening before Jack arrived at the hospital. He had spent long hours tucked away in a corner of the reference section of the library while the stock-take went on around him. The computer had been down, so he had to rely on old-fashioned methods to dig out the books he thought might be helpful.

Lychford in the seventeenth century. There had been several books. Local history books full of detailed information – none of which moved Jack a single step nearer to learning anything about the Hilliard family. Or if they had even existed outside Tom's head.

Most of the books contained illustrations: line drawings and antique, blurred woodcuts. The primitive nature of the angular pictures served to make the images all the more unsettling. Grinning skeletons stalked empty streets. Priests bent over deathbeds, giving last rites. The plague, personified as a stooped and hooded man carrying a scythe across his shoulders, prowled the night. Doctors, cloaked and cowled, wore curious pointed masks, filled with the flowers and herbs intended to ward off the sickness. They looked to Jack like large and grotesque birds.

The plague had been brought to Lychford by people fleeing London, that much Jack now knew. Wretched refugees flooded out of the suffering metropolis, and the disease came with them like a dark cloud. Like the grim miasma of Darryl's bizarre stories.

But there was no reference to be found concerning a family named Hilliard. There was no real reason why there should be. Not in the local library.

Jack wondered whether he might be allowed access to the parish records. The Hilliards might be found there, if the records went back far enough and were intact.

Jack found his father sitting at Tom's bedside. There was a magazine open on his father's lap, but the man's quiet eyes were on the face of his sleeping son.

'Hello, Dad,' Jack whispered.

His father made a gesture of acknowledgement. He stood up and padded across the floor to where Jack stood.

'He's been up-and-down a bit,' said Mr Christmas, his mouth close to Jack's ear. 'A bit restless. I think he's been dreaming. He's just quietened down.'

'Is he any better?' asked Jack. 'Have you managed to speak to the doctor?'

'I had a quick word with Dr Fairfax before he went off duty,' whispered Mr Christmas. 'He's not back on call until tomorrow evening, now.'

'Has Tom said anything about why he went peculiar?' Jack was referring to the incident earlier that day with the glass of water.

'The doctor says it's just part of Tom feeling unwell,' said Mr Christmas.

'Do they know what's wrong yet?'

'They think they've found out what's *not* wrong with him,' said Mr Christmas. He steered Jack out into the corridor. He quietly closed the door.

'That's better,' he said. 'We can talk now.'

Jack frowned at him. 'They know what it *isn't?*' he said. 'What's the good of that?'

'They have to eliminate possibilities, Jack,' said

Mr Christmas. 'Like, they needed to eliminate cholera, for instance.'

'Cholera?' Jack gasped. 'They thought he had cholera? That's bad, isn't it?'

'Calm down, Jack. Some of the symptoms were similar to cholera – and you do get cholera from contaminated water. They needed to check it out. But it isn't cholera. That's certain. And they've done a test for Weil's disease, too. That's caused by water that rats have . . . um . . . been in.'

'Rats?'

'Apparently,' said Mr Christmas. 'Not very pleasant. But they don't think Tom has Weil's disease either.'

'Have they done a test for bubonic plague?'

Mr Christmas laughed. Then he saw that Jack wasn't joking. He put an arm around Jack's shoulders. 'I don't think your brother has bubonic plague, Jack.' He looked into Jack's eyes. 'Is that what you've been worrying about? I know it was nasty down in that cellar, but those people had been dead for over three hundred years, Jack. I don't think they'd still be contagious.'

'No.' Jack smiled. 'No, of course not. But I couldn't help thinking—'

'Well, don't,' said Mr Christmas. 'At least, not daft stuff like that. Tom's feeling rotten because he swallowed a lot of filthy water. He'll be up and about in no time. You'll see.' Mr Christmas squeezed Jack's shoulders and gave a reassuring smile. 'Now then, do you want to take over for a while and let me get off home for some dinner? I haven't eaten for hours. My stomach thinks my throat's been cut.'

Jack sat quietly at the side of the bed. Tom's eyes

were moving under his lids. It looked very strange. REM sleep. The sleep that produces dreams.

Jack picked up his father's magazine. *The Landscape Gardener.* Mm, exciting!

Jack didn't exactly hear anything. He just felt that something had changed in the room. He looked at Tom and saw that his brother's eyes were open.

'Hello there,' said Jack. 'You just saved me from having to start reading one of Dad's trade mags. How's it going?'

'I had a dream,' Tom said. His voice was faint but clear. He frowned. 'Or . . . maybe I had someone else's dream . . .'

'Sorry?'

Tom shook his head. 'I dunno. Don't ask.' His brain was clearing now. He didn't want to talk about the repellent dream. He'd rather it faded quietly away. He was concerned that he might somehow anchor it too close to reality if he built it up into a structure of words.

Jack smiled. 'So? Chucked any water over anyone recently?'

'Not recently,' said Tom.

'Do you remember doing it?'

'Yes.'

'Any idea why?'

Tom gave a small shrug. 'I just had a feeling,' he said. 'A funny feeling. I dunno. You'll think I've gone barmy.'

'More than likely. Tell me, anyway.'

'I thought . . . well, I thought it was poison. Don't ask me why.'

'It was water.'

'Yes. I know.' He gave a lopsided grin. 'I've gone

bonkers in the head, Jack. Go on, I bet everyone's talking about it. Tom's finally gone potty. I bet they are.'

'Not to me, they aren't,' said Jack. 'Do you remember all that stuff you told Regan? The Will Hilliard stuff?'

'No. I told you. I don't remember it at all.'

'I've been doing some research,' said Jack. 'I've been trying to find out if there really were any people called Hilliard living around here in the past.'

Tom's eyes widened. 'You think this Will Hilliard bloke might be . . .' he made a tentative gesture towards his head, ' . . . a real person . . . in *there?*'

'Well, it's not a place *I'd* want to visit,' Jack said, smiling. 'But it might be one explanation for how you're behaving.'

Tom rested back into the pillows, his eyes open but vague. 'I wonder what the people in this place would make of that idea,' he said softly.

'Ask them,' said Jack.

A half-grin. 'Then they'd be certain I was barmy,' said Tom. 'They'd throw away the key.' He looked at Jack. 'Did you find anything?'

'Plenty. But nothing to explain what's going on with you.'

'Tell me, anyway,' said Tom. 'It's not like I've got anywhere much to go.'

'Well, I know tons of stuff about the plague now. For a start the Great Plague of London was just the last big outbreak of a disease which had been killing people all over Europe for centuries. Going right back to the fourteenth century.'

'The Black Death!' said Tom. 'I remember that from history.'

'Yup, that's the one. Anyway, I'd always thought that the plague was wiped out by the Great Fire of London. But that's not what happened at all. Truth is, no one really knows why the plague went away. Here, I've made some notes.' Jack yanked a battered old notebook out of his back pocket. He grinned at his brother. 'Are you sitting comfortably? Then I'll begin . . .'

'Frankie? How long are you planning on being in there? I need to give Tabitha her bath!'

Frankie came out of a rushing daydream. She was in the shower, under a fierce, cleansing cascade of hot water. She had no idea how long she'd been in there. She had needed the flood of water to wash away the memory of the bell.

Dizzy as if from deep sleep, Frankie pawed for the control dial and turned the water off. She shoved the cubicle door open. The bathroom was full of fine grey water vapour. The mirror was an opaque sheet of hammered iron.

'Coming!' she called. It had been Samantha's voice at the bathroom door.

Frankie wrapped herself in a large towel and drew back the bolt.

Samantha was standing there with Tabitha hanging off her arm. 'About time!' Samantha pushed past her. 'There's wet all over the floor. Someone could slip and hurt themselves. How often have I told you about putting the mat down? Frankie?'

But Frankie was already back in her room. She

looked at the time. It was a quarter to nine in the evening. Her reverie in the shower must have lasted at least an hour – maybe even longer. She'd intended to go and see Jack, but time had run away with her. He wouldn't still be in the library. He'd be home. Or at the hospital.

She dragged a brush through her wet hair. She could go and visit Tom again. Jack might even be there. If not, she could always phone him later. See what he'd found out. Maybe tell him about the bell? Or maybe not.

If she got a move on, she could be ready in a few minutes. It was still so warm out there that her hair would dry in the wind if she went on her bike. Yeah, why not?

It was a couple of minutes before nine o'clock. Frankie ran downstairs and stuck her damp head in through the front room doorway. Her father was watching television.

'I'm going to visit Tom.'

Her father stared up at the wall clock. 'Isn't it a bit late?'

'It's still light out,' said Frankie. 'I won't be long. I'll use the bike. I just want to say hello. I promised.' Not true, but it sounded good.

'You be careful, then,' said her father. 'Straight there and back. And don't forget to put your lights on.'

'I won't.'

'Home by ten, or there'll be trouble. Right?'

It wouldn't take more than twenty minutes to get there. Twenty minutes with Tom. Twenty minutes back. Just right. Easy.

'Righty-ho! See you later.'

The clocks all over Lychford were striking the hour of nine as Frankie wheeled her bike out into the road and climbed on board.

The hospital was only a twenty-minute ride away. Frankie never got there.

CHAPTER TEN
Atishoo! Atishoo!
We All Fall Down

Tom lay back with half-closed eyes. The world was hazy, but not in an unpleasant way, and there was the comforting sound of Jack's voice to moor him to reality.

'In 1665, the Mayor of Lychford got together with some local bigwigs and imposed a nine p.m. curfew.' Jack was reading from his scribbled notes. 'Apparently, people who had the plague were locked up in their houses all day. After nine o'clock at night, all the healthy people had to stay indoors and the plague victims were allowed to walk about and get some fresh air.'

'I see,' murmured Tom. 'Nice for them.' He laughed softly. 'Night life, I suppose!'

It was seven minutes past nine o'clock.

The hem of the sky was livid with scraps and slivers of cloud, dyed orange and sour yellow and a grizzly, lurid red by the setting sun. Frankie cycled past the ghost-white sheet of St Jude's church. The air was as still and thick as treacle. She was sweating and trembling. At any moment she dreaded the sound of that bell.

This was an awful, *awful* idea! Turn around and go home. No. Coward. Face it. Get past the church and it'll all be fine. You'll see.

Above her the sky was a tight cap of swarming blue – like a crystal lid over the world. Screwed down over Lychford, eliminating breathable air.

She pushed down on the pedals, but the effort was immense. The road to the hospital reared before her like a tidal wave.

She saw someone stumbling along the pavement. Someone who walked with a stooped shuffle, arms huddled to the chest. Wearing rags. As she watched, the person staggered sideways and leaned one arm on a tree. The head hung. Frankie heard weak coughing.

She stopped her bike.

'Excuse me? Are you OK?' She walked the bike in under the shade of the tree. 'Can I help?'

The face lifted.

The mouth grinned from a wound of ravaged purple. A low laugh came from the mouth. Humourless. Desperate. A scrawny, purple-hued hand reached out.

A blast of foul breath came with that terrible laughter. Frankie backed away, almost falling as her legs became entangled with her bike.

Then the figure was gone.

Frankie had no sense of the moment when the palsied shape winked out of existence. It was simply *there*, and then it was as if it had *never* been there.

A disgusting smell hung in the air.

Frankie stared around her. Now there were scores

of shrouded, ragged figures moving all around her, stirring the dense twilight.

She felt sick and weak.

Lunatic laughter razor-slashed the darkening street.

A claw-like hand reached out towards her.

She fell backwards and her bike hit the road with a sound like the clashing of knives.

Jack flipped over the next page of his notebook. 'Oh, yes,' he said. 'Here's something really interesting. Like, for instance, did you know that the nursery rhyme *Ring a ring o' roses* is all to do with the plague?'

'Is it?' asked Tom. 'How come?'

'Well, the line *Ring a ring o' roses* refers to the red pock-marks that broke out on people's skin when they got the plague,' said Jack. 'And the line *a pocket full of posies* is to do with the fact that people carried posies of flowers around with them to ward off the horrible smell of the plague victims.'

'And *Atishoo, atishoo?*' asked Tom.

'The early symptoms were a bit like flu, apparently,' Jack explained. 'Sneezing and so on.'

'Right. I see,' said Tom. 'And I suppose *We all fall down* is pretty obvious.'

'Yup. All fall down,' said Jack. '*Dead*!'

*

Ring a ring o' roses, a pocket full of posies,
Atishoo! Atishoo! We all fall down!

Regan's concentration was shaken loose by the

chanting voices of what sounded like a dozen or more little kids. The wall blocks came crashing down on the small screen of her Gameboy. Tetris. The highest level. It took all her concentration to keep up with the speed of the game on that setting.

The shrill, faint children's voices had broken the thread.

'Rats!'

She was sitting cross-legged in the middle of her bed. Across the room the television was on with the sound down. MTV. She liked the punchy kaleidoscope of multi-coloured images that flashed across the screen on that channel, but most of the music they played was really skanky! Regan only really liked hard-core techno-hip-hop. Everything else was skanky to the max!

The king has sent his daughter, to fetch a pail of water,
Atishoo! Atishoo! We all fall down!

Regan stared at the window. Outside, the evening was just bleeding into night. Clouds hung low in the sky like blood-stained fragments of bandage.

Kids playing outside? Singing? No, that couldn't be right. The grounds of this house were, like, immense. What kids?

The bird upon the steeple, sits high above the people,
Atishoo! Atishoo! We all fall down!

Regan scrambled up off the bed, trying to home in on where exactly the singing was coming from. Sometimes it seemed to drift in from outside, and sometimes it was like it came from within the house itself.

She yanked her bedroom door open.

The wedding bells are ringing, the boys and girls are
   singing,
Atishoo! Atishoo! We all fall down!

The voices were coming from downstairs.

'Hey!' Regan hollered. 'Jennie! Turn the sound down, man!'

The cows are in the meadow, lying fast asleep,
Atishoo! Atishoo! We all fall down – dead!

The voices broke into peals and squeals of laughter.

Regan frowned. It must be the television. But it sure didn't sound like voices coming over a TV speaker. It sounded for all the world like Jennie had invited a whole bunch of local kids in to play games down there.

There was some general shouting and yelling, and then the song began again.

Ring a ring o' roses, a pocket full of posies,
Atishoo! Atishoo! We all fall down!

Regan walked slowly down the stairs. The smell of vinegar drifted on the air. Regan felt dizzy. The walls of the stairwell and of the wide hall beyond shimmered as though in a kind of heat-haze.

The door to the living room was closed. The voices came from within. Regan could feel the faint vibrations of feet stamping in time to the rhythm of the wild singing.

The air thickened around her. Sweat trickled out of her hair.

The voices became louder. Ten kids. Twenty kids, maybe. She could almost see them. Hands clasping hands as they sang and stamped and spun in frantic rings.

Something was wrong.

Regan felt as if her movements were slowing down. It seemed to take for ever to get across the tiled floor of the hall and reach the bare-wood door to the living room. She watched her own arm as it reached out for the door handle. It was like looking at an arm that belonged to someone else.

The gap between thinking and acting widened. Reality plummeted into the gulf. Regan saw the hallway twist and distort around her. The door shrank away and then blew out towards her, as if the room were breathing.

She stared at her fingers as they crept imperceptibly towards the brass door handle. She'd never touch it. She'd never reach it.

Atishoo! Atishoo! We all fall down – dead!

The singing and dancing reached a crescendo. There were shouts and screams of laughter and thuds, as if the rings of singers that circled in Regan's mind had broken up and the children had gone tumbling to the floor.

The door was disfigured by a rough cross of red paint. Red dripped onto Regan's hand. Warm as blood.

She gripped the handle and pushed the door open.

The voices were swept away on a wind from nowhere.

In the living room, Jennie was sprawled on the couch, watching television. A game show. Apart from the shifting images on the television screen, there was no movement in the room.

Jennie gave Regan a bored glance. '*Wheel of Fortune*'s on, if you're interested,' she drawled. 'You've missed half of it. Some guy just won fifteen hundred pounds.'

Regan stared slowly around the room like someone shaken roughly out of deep sleep.

She could still smell the vinegar.

'Most of the doctors at the time were convinced the plague was caused by bad air,' said Jack. 'They were really into how bad everything smelled around plague victims. They even reckoned that where the plague was at its worst, the air was so thick with it, that it'd put fires out.'

'So they just locked people away in their houses until they died,' said Tom. 'Charming.'

'There were a few plague hospitals,' said Jack. 'They were called pest houses. There was one in Lychford, but the book didn't say where exactly. The really bad thing about locking people up in infected houses was that everyone in the house would be quarantined, even if only one person had symptoms.'

'Nice one,' sighed Tom. 'So even if you were clear to start off with, you'd catch it off the infected people because you couldn't get away from them. Brilliant!'

'People were terrified of the disease,' said Jack. 'I suppose you can't blame them. They thought the sickness came out of dead people's eyes and straight into the eyes of living people. There was one theory that you could actually see the bad air hanging around the heads of victims, like some kind of weird halo. And some people said that the plague was a cloaked man on a big black horse, laying waste to everything in his path . . .'

The milling figures seemed unaware of Frankie as she lay gasping in the road. One wheel of her fallen bike turned slowly. Purple night was seeping up the sky. The tall trees were black. She heard laughter and the hammer of running feet. Shouts. Yellow flames coiled in the distance. Someone fell and the constantly moving figures slid away.

She sat up. The stench was unbearable. She crouched in the road, one hand over her nose and mouth, the other reaching out for her bike.

A light grew at the far end of the road. It crawled, green as poison, along the tarmac. At the heart of the sickly light Frankie could see a fist of darkness. She could hear the slow percussion of hooves. *Clop. Clop. Clop. Clop.*

The deformed people shambled away from the growing light. The rags of their clothing trailed after them as they fled, moaning and whimpering, slumping into shadows and creeping away into corners and crevices.

Frankie stared at the expanding core of darkness. She narrowed her eyes. The horrible lurid green light made it difficult to guess the shape.

Clop. Clop. Clop. Clop.

A man on a horse. Frankie squinted against the glare.

A wide-sweeping cloak. A curiously-shaped helmet. One arm lifted and bent, holding a standard. A forked pennant hung limp.

The horse devoured the road. The light flared on the trees. The face of St Jude's church glowed like a hideous skull.

Frankie shrank. The slow beat of the hooves was deafening. She could hear laborious breathing. The horseman loomed over her. Towering. Immense. Unearthly.

The helmet was surrounded by a pale light. Maggot-white eyes glowed in darkness.

If the horse lifted one of its colossal hooves and brought it down, she would be crushed into the ground.

The horseman lowered the standard and pointed it at her. The pennant dragged on the road.

Trembling, Frankie clambered to her feet.

She swallowed.

The huge shape loomed over her.

'You aren't real.' Her voice shook. In the immensity of the impossible night, it sounded thin and brittle. But she had managed to get the words out.

'You are not real!'

She closed her eyes against the monstrous light and lunged blindly forwards with both arms stretched out.

'Not real! Not real! Not! Not! *Not*!'

She fell, grazing the heels of her hands.

Twilight filled the tree-lined well of the road. Street lights gleamed. The air smelled of flowers. The tower of St Jude's was as white as snow.

One wheel turned slowly on her fallen bike.

The evil had gone.

Frankie picked her bike up. She turned it homewards. She cycled slowly towards the roundabout and the long, gentle rise of Lawrence Hill.

She didn't look back.

'So, there really wasn't any kind of cure for the plague?' Tom asked. 'Nothing at all?'

Jack shook his head. 'Listen,' he said. 'I wrote this bit out in full.' He read from his scrawled notes. 'It is the most terrible of diseases, for when anyone who is infected by it dies, all who see him in his sickness, or visit him, or do any business with him, or even carry him to the grave, quickly follow him thither, and there is no known means of protection.'

'Yeah, well, that sounds pretty final,' said Tom.

'The only thing people could protect themselves from was the horrible stink,' said Jack. 'Apparently the plague victims smelled like nothing on earth.'

'What did they do?' asked Tom. 'Squirt them with de-plague-orant?'

'Not quite,' said Jack. 'People used to carry posies of flowers around. You know: as in, *a pocket full of posies*. Or if they couldn't get flowers, they'd use other things. Herbs and spices. And there was stuff called Plague Water which you drank as a kind of antidote. Oh, and another favourite anti-stinky thing, believe it or not, was vinegar.'

Regan leaned low over the basin and splashed her face over and over again with the cold water as it ran fresh from the tap. Her hair hung in thick black tendrils from her forehead, the ends like rat-tails in the clear water.

She was still pretty badly shaken.

The singing of those non-existent children had been so eerie. And she didn't much like the way the house had kind of *warped* around her, either. I mean, a joke's a joke, guys. But let's not go insane around here!

The smell of vinegar permeated everything. Even her mother's most expensive, exclusive French perfume – from a bottle she'd found on the shelf – even that smelled like vinegar. And this time the smell just wouldn't go away.

Regan dunked her face in the pool of crystal water. She counted to twenty before rising for air. She savagely wrenched the tap, ending the flow of water. She gripped the sides of the basin and hung her head.

'Aww, Jeez!' she whispered. 'What's happening to me?'

She lifted her hooded eyes and stared into the wall mirror.

The face that stared back at her was blotched with red weals, the skin grey and sallow, the eyes sunken and feverish in dark sockets.

She opened her mouth to scream. Blood dribbled over her lips. Her teeth were red.

The room convulsed around her and everything went black.

CHAPTER ELEVEN
Shadows on a Summer's Day

Jack sat alone at the breakfast bar in the kitchen and stared out at the crooked old oak tree. He was puzzled.

The morning had begun with a frantic phone call from Regan. She wouldn't say what the problem was. She just said: 'Don't move a muscle! I'm coming over!'

Jack had moved enough muscles to fix himself breakfast. Dad was already on the road, heading up north to check out the new landscaping job he'd won. Mum was scrabbling her things together for a long day at the library.

The front door slammed behind her. The battered Morris Minor coughed and spluttered before the engine ignited. The phone rang again.

Jack picked the receiver up. 'Now what?' He assumed it was Regan once more. Frantic phone call part two. Through the frosted-glass door-panel he saw the blobby green car go trundling down the road.

'Eh? What? Jack? Is that you?'

'Oh. Sorry, Frankie. I thought it was Regan.'

'No, it's not Regan. It's me. Listen.' His friend's voice was urgent, almost breathless. 'I need to see you. I'll come over right away. Don't go anywhere.'

'What's up?'

'I'll tell you when I get there.'

And the line went dead.

So, Jack sat and waited and gazed at the tree. Puzzled.

They arrived within two minutes of each other.

The three friends went out and sat on the lawn. Jack could see that the two girls were agitated. Both of them had something in their heads that was frightening them. He got the impression of coiled serpents, clamped behind their eyes.

'OK, guys,' Regan said in a low voice. 'I wanna tell you what happened to me last night.' Her bright blue eyes moved from one to the other. 'And I don't want either of you to say a word until I've finished.' She spoke very precisely. 'Even if it sounds totally crazy.'

She told them everything. Slowly, hesitantly, she recreated that unnerving evening.

' . . . then I guess I must have fainted,' she said. 'Me! And I never faint. I woke up on the floor in the bathroom.' She shivered. 'I didn't bother taking another look in the mirror, I can tell you that! I just got out of there and locked myself in my room.' She let out a long breath. 'Nothing else happened.' She straightened up. 'OK, guys. Break it to me gently – am I freaking out or what?'

'Before we go to a vote on that,' Frankie said solemnly, 'I think you need to hear what was happening to me at the same time.'

Birds darted in among the trees. Distant traffic murmured on the roads. Scuds of thin cloud passed across the sky. Someone shouted in a nearby garden. A radio played pop music. A DJ babbled. Birds flew. Cloud veiled the sun.

Frankie finished recounting her experiences. The three friends looked at one another.

No one spoke.

The sky pressed down on the garden like a giant sweating hand.

'So-o-o-o.' Regan couldn't stand the silence any longer. 'Anyone got any theories?'

'Something came out of the plague pit,' Jack said. 'Something escaped. It . . . I don't know . . . it infected us, somehow. Tom worst of all, but us as well.'

'Have *you* seen any weird things?' Frankie asked him.

Jack shook his head.

'Nothing?' asked Regan.

'Nothing.'

'So, what is it?' asked Regan. 'Some kind of creepy brain-virus? I mean, all this stuff – it isn't real, is it? We're just imagining it, right?'

'The horseman vanished when I tried to touch him,' Frankie said. 'I think that must mean he was just in my mind. A hallucination.'

'I sure hope you're right,' said Regan. 'The question is – how do we get this junk out of our minds? Jack – you're the one with the kooky brain. What's the usual way of getting freaky stuff out of your head?'

Jack gazed into the distance.

'Uh, Jack,' said Regan. She flapped a hand in

front of his face. 'We could use a little help, here, man.'

He looked at her. 'What makes you think I can do anything?'

Regan looked surprised. 'Your famous sixth-sense thing?'

Jack laughed softly. Sadly. 'I've told you and told you: I can't control it. I can't *use* it. If I could, don't you think I'd have warned Tom to keep away from the pit? Things happen in my head, or they don't. That's it. End of story.'

'And nothing's happening now?' Frankie asked gently. 'Nothing at all?'

'Nothing at all,' Jack repeated.

'Terrific,' murmured Regan.

'I don't think we should panic,' said Frankie.

Regan snorted with laughter. 'Who's panicking? I'm still in shock! You'll know when I reach panic. That's when I start running round and round the garden screaming and ripping my hair out in clumps.'

'Tom's the key to all this,' Jack said. 'The things you two are experiencing are just . . .' He shook his head. 'Well, they're nasty and frightening, but they don't seem to have any kind of purpose. Beyond scaring you stupid, I mean. It's like worst nightmares come real.' He looked at them. 'Do you see what I mean? There's no reason behind the things that have happened to you two. It's just random nastiness.'

'But Tom seems to be caught up in something a lot more specific,' said Frankie. 'Yeah, I *do* see what you mean.'

'So, Tom got the direct hit, and we're just suffering from the fallout,' said Regan. 'Is that it?'

'Something like that,' said Jack. 'I think maybe Will Hilliard is using Tom to try and get some kind of message across.'

'Fine,' said Regan. 'Let's go ask him what he wants. Then maybe things can get back to normal around here.'

'I don't think he'll talk to all of us,' Jack said. He looked at Regan. 'You're the one he likes.'

'Don't be so sure,' said Regan. 'Last I heard, he thought I was some kind of demon from hell.'

'Then you've got to convince him you're not,' said Jack.

Frankie nodded. 'You've got to convince him that you really are his sister Jane. He'll open up, then. I bet.'

Regan looked dubiously at them. 'I dunno, guys. What if I mess up?'

'You won't,' said Jack.

Regan raised a quizzical eyebrow. 'Wanna bet?'

'Uh . . . hi . . . there.' Regan smiled at Tom from the doorway of his hospital room. He was lying quietly in bed. A magazine lay open at his side. Unread. He was looking out of the window.

His head turned at the sound of Regan's voice.

'How's it going?' she asked through the fixed smile. 'Alive and kickin' . . . or . . . or . . . uh . . . not?'

Tom stared at her. His face was completely blank.

Jack and Frankie were keeping out of sight in the corridor. Regan gave Jack an uneasy glance. He flicked his head, urging her to go into the room.

She stepped over the threshold.

On the way over to the hospital they had put a lot of thought into what Regan should say once she was alone in the room with Tom. How best could she draw Will Hilliard out?

The smile still cemented onto her face, Regan walked to the bedside. She wasn't at all sure about this. Truth was, she felt kind of stupid.

'You ... you're looking a whole lot better ... uh ... Will,' she said. 'Uh ... the doctor says you'll be just fine in a couple of days.'

Tom lifted his hand towards her. Her first reaction was to swat it away, but instead she took his hand in hers and gave it a squeeze. His hand was hot and sticky. Limp like raw meat.

Regan sat on the very edge of the bed. Tom lay gazing at her.

The silence became unnerving.

'So ...' Regan began. 'You've been real sick ... Will. Do you wanna tell me about it?'

Tom frowned, as if he couldn't quite understand her.

'Jane?' he whispered.

'Uh-huh.' His eyes showed confusion. 'Yes,' said Regan. 'That's right. I'm Jane.'

His fingers tightened for a moment around her hand. 'I am glad,' he murmured.

That was part one of the mission accomplished. She'd made the link. Now came the tricky bit.

'Will?' she said softly. 'The doctors think you'll get better a whole lot quicker if you talk some.'

He stared glassily at her.

'Talk?' she said. 'Talk about yourself? Uh ... about us. About the family.' She squeezed his hand. 'You're

Will Hilliard. I'm Jane Hilliard,' she prompted. 'I'm your sister, yeah? So, who else is there, Will?'

'Papa,' said Tom. 'There is Papa.'

'And what does he do?'

A confused frown. 'Nicholas will become a partner in the Company when he comes of age.'

'The Company, huh, Will? What does the Company do? Does it make stuff? Sell stuff?'

Tom's fingers gripped, pinching Regan's hand. 'You must tell them,' he whispered, his voice hoarse and urgent. 'You must warn them, Jane. You must warn them of Dr Bludworth.' He lifted his head from the pillows. His eyes glowed. 'Dr Bludworth means to kill us, Jane. He means to kill us all.'

CHAPTER TWELVE
Plague Water

The room was panelled with dark wood. A portrait hung over the fireplace. Papa. A very important man in Lychford. Mr Charles Hilliard. Importer of textiles. A merchant of distinction, renowned throughout the south of England. A man who had met the King. Charles II. In person.

The room glowed with sunlight but a veiled terror poisoned the air. The terror beat on the walls of the house. It gnawed the walls and nested in the roof-beams. It rattled at the latch and clawed at the windows. Beady, blood-bright eyes peered through cracks. Needle-sharp teeth snapped.

Jane sat on a carved oak chest, gazing anxiously out through a trefoil window. Her clothes were plain but well-cut. Her hair hung like black water down her back. Wide, pale forehead. Full of thoughts. Jane Hilliard.

Papa sat at his desk, tapping impatient fingers. Often he would stare over at the long-case clock. Waiting for a tardy arrival. The expected guest was over two hours late. The fear was that he might not come at all.

Mama and Molly sat in white window-light and sewed with a kind of concentration that suggested their suppressed burden of concern and apprehension. Nicholas stood, a young man, first-born, ramrod stiff, his back to the fireplace, hands knotted together.

'He will not come,' Nicholas muttered. 'Not now. It is too late.'

Silence. Jane glanced at him and bit down on her lower lip.

'He will come.' Papa's voice rumbled like distant thunder. 'He said he would come. He will come.'

Framed needlework samplers lined the walls: the twelve good rules of Charles I. Brought out from dusty corners after the Restoration. Court fans lay upon the mahogany panelling like great sleeping moths. Molly shifted position in her roundabout chair and lifted her eyes to glance out into the deserted street.

He will not come.

A bell rattled away downstairs.

Papa let out a sigh, his head dipping into his hand.

All eyes moved to the door.

A maid showed the doctor into the room. With him came an air of urgency and haste. He removed his cloak with a swooping flourish. He waited until the maid had left before speaking.

Papa rose and clasped the doctor's hands.

'I was detained.' The doctor's face was cragged and scored like a moorland outcrop. His hair was iron-grey. His eyes a dark brown that was almost black.

'You are here,' said Papa. 'Praise be!'

'Praise be, indeed,' the doctor said gravely. 'In these times, to reach the end of the day with a sound body is cause enough for praise.'

'How many have died?' Papa asked.

'I cannot say. Too many. And there is no abatement. They are digging a pit in Tanner's Yard. It will fill too swiftly, I fear.'

'Dr Bludworth!' Mama's voice was balanced on the margin of hysteria. 'Do you have the remedy?'

The doctor turned to her and gave a brief bow. 'I do,' he said. He drew a small earthenware flask from among his clothes. It had a cork stopper and was coated with a green glaze. He held it up like the Grail. 'Drink of this plague water and the sickness will pass you by. You must all drink. It has protected me well.' His eyes turned back to Papa. 'Do you have the money?'

'I do.' Papa opened a drawer in his desk and took out a bag of coins. The transaction complete, the doctor swaddled himself again in his cloak and left the room, as though afraid of spending too long breathing the same air as the gathered family.

At the door he turned and swept the room with his eyes. 'Drink!' he said. 'Drink deep and be of good cheer. And may it deliver you from all fear.' A ragged smile cracked his face. 'Drink hearty, my friends, and you will not die of the plague – you have my word on that.'

The door clicked shut and the doctor was gone.

Papa walked over to Mama and urged her to drink. Molly drank next. She grimaced in distaste.

Jane cried out in disgust as the liquid rolled over her tongue. Nicholas swigged and then stood tight-lipped.

Lastly Papa brought the flask over to Will, who had been sitting quietly in a corner.

'Drink, boy.'

Will shook his head, his lips compressed.

'Do not be foolish! Drink! We all must drink!'

Will took a mouthful of the plague water. It was thick and bitter and sour. He pretended to swallow. While Papa drank from the flask, Will walked calmly from the room and spat the stuff out unseen.

He didn't like the doctor. There was no reason for it. Will Hilliard loathed the man with all his heart; loathed his rugged face and his quick, mal-evolent dark eyes.

Papa gathered the servants together and allowed each of them a mouthful of the plague water.

That night Molly awoke sweating and sick.

The house was in turmoil.

Mama became ill.

At first light the searcher came. She diagnosed the plague.

Nicholas fell ill.

The house was locked up and a warden stood guard night and day. Food and medicine was allowed in. The servants began to fall ill.

Papa showed no sign of the illness. On the third day, he fell like a great oak and was dead within hours, his face and hands turned a livid purple.

Mama died the following day.

Jane fought the disease like a wild cat. It took her all the same.

The servants began to die.

Will hid himself away, gnawing dry bread and drinking stale water.

The house became still. The last of the wrenching coughing stopped at midnight on the fifth day.

Will huddled in his hiding place when the wardens came to take the bodies to the great pit in Tanner's Yard. If they found him, they would surely take him to the pest house, and he would die there.

In the cold hour before dawn, Dr Bludworth came alone to the deserted house. Will followed him secretly and silently as he moved from room to room, ransacking the place for anything of value. When he slipped Mama's jewellery into his deep sack, Will could almost have leaped on him and clawed his face with his fingernails.

The plague water had been poisoned. Dr Bludworth had murdered Will's entire family and was now reaping the rewards of his terrible crime. After all, who would question nine more deaths when all the town was dying?

Will fled the house and hammered on his neighbour's door.

They listened to his story. They came to the Hilliards' house. They discovered Dr Bludworth in Papa's study, a black sack of plunder at his feet, drinking Papa's finest brandywine.

Justice and vengeance clapped swift and hard down upon the murderer. There was no trial. Will found the flask of poison and brought it to them. There were still a few drops left. They forced the doctor to drink. Then they locked him in the death house and waited.

Five days later they brought his ravaged body out and threw it into the plague pit in Tanner's Yard.

Men swore that his eyes snapped open as they began to heave the soil down into the brimming pit. They said he was buried alive.

Will hoped that it was true.

'Whoo, boy!'

It was a couple of minutes before Regan pulled herself together sufficiently to do anything other than just sit in silence on the edge of Tom's bed, holding his hand and staring at his face.

His eyes had been closed throughout the extraordinary narrative. As the story had unfolded, his voice had become softer and softer until, at the end, it was no more than a breath.

Now there was only the breathing, slow and deep.

Tom was asleep.

Gently, Regan eased her fingers out of his. Hot and clammy. Yuck! She wiped her hand on her hip.

Jack and Frankie came quietly into the room.

She looked up at them. Judging by the expressions on their faces, they'd heard the whole incredible story. Regan assumed she looked as stunned as her two friends.

Jack briefly touched Tom's arm, then gestured for the three of them to leave the room.

There was the usual hospital bustle in the corridor: people coming and going, trolleys being wheeled, an elderly woman with a walking-frame.

'Well?' said Regan. 'What did you make of that?' She was just about beginning to recover from Tom's story.

'We can't talk here,' said Jack.

They walked towards the lift. The metal doors slid open.

'Rhea!' Frankie said in surprise.

The young woman stepped out of the lift. She was carrying flowers. Her eyes were obscured by sunglasses.

'I brought these for him,' she said. 'How is he?'

'Sleeping,' said Jack.

Rhea gave a rueful smile. 'I don't suppose he'd have wanted to see me, anyway,' she said. 'I just felt like I had to make the effort. You know?'

'Give them here,' said Frankie. 'I don't expect it'll wake him up if I just pop them in for him.' She smiled at Rhea. 'It was a nice thought.'

Rhea handed her the flowers and Frankie headed back to Tom's room.

Rhea sighed. 'So? How's it going?'

'Apparently they know what he *doesn't* have,' said Regan. 'Problem is, they don't know what he *does* have. Great, huh?'

'Still?' said Rhea. 'God! These things take an age, don't they?'

'It feels like it,' said Jack.

'Now I'm here, would you like to go somewhere for a cup of coffee or a coke or something?' Rhea suggested. 'There's a café down near the main entrance. My treat.'

'I have to get home,' Jack said. 'Sorry.'

'Me, too,' said Regan. 'Things to do. My mom's having a reception for the prime minister of Saudi Arabia, and it takes for ever to get dolled up for that kind of bash. Drag, huh?'

Rhea looked surprised. 'Yes. I suppose so.' She shrugged. 'Never mind. Another time, eh?'

'Certainly,' said Regan. 'Looking forward to it.'

Frankie came out of the side room. 'He didn't wake up,' she said.

'Rhea was talking about us all going to the café,' Jack said quickly. 'But I told her we had things to do.'

Frankie caught on. 'Oh, yeah. I have to baby-sit.' She looked at her watch for added emphasis. 'I'm already late.'

'No problem,' said Rhea. 'Oh! There was one thing I thought might interest you. I know you've got better things on your mind right now, but I've been doing some local research.' She curled her lip. 'Truth is, I'm trying to get back into Professor Paulson's good books. The thing is, I was looking up some old documentation from the seventeenth century – you know, from the time when the . . . um . . . the pit was dug. Guess what? It turns out that this hospital was built on the very same site as the old pest house.' She smiled. 'Isn't that interesting?'

Rhea went with them down to the hospital reception area. The three friends did their best not to reveal the thoughts that were boiling in their heads. They knew better than to discuss those kinds of thoughts in front of outsiders.

They waved to Rhea as she climbed into her car.

They waited until she had nosed the car out into the traffic.

'Can we talk about this now,' said Regan. 'Or would you prefer for my brain to just explode right here?'

A taxi drew up and they had to move out of the way.

'Not here,' said Jack.

'Where?' asked Frankie.

'My place,' said Regan. 'It's closest. Face-ache's gone to London for a shopping frenzy. She won't be back till they shut down for the night. We won't be disturbed.'

They assumed Face-ache was Jennie.

'I thought you said your mum was having some kind of do?' said Jack.

Regan grinned. 'Was I that convincing? Neat! Actually, she is seeing the Saudi Arabian geezer-in-chief, but they're having their pow-wow up in London.'

'Oh, hello!' Frankie said suddenly. 'Isn't that Dr Fairfax?' They followed the line of her eyes. 'Perhaps he'll have some news.' The doctor was standing talking to someone at a side entrance a little way off. Even as Jack and Regan looked around, he climbed into a blue BMW and slammed the door.

'Looks like he's off,' said Frankie. 'You'd better be quick if you want a word with him.'

Jack trotted along to where the big car was parked. He waved at the doctor through the windscreen. The window glided down.

'Hello there,' said the doctor as the three friends gathered by the car.

'Sorry to bother you like this,' said Jack. 'I just wondered if you had any news?'

'Sorry, John,' said the doctor. Jack didn't bother correcting him. 'I'm not on call until this evening. I wouldn't even be here now, but I had to have a quick word with someone.' The doctor smiled. 'Don't worry about Tom,' he said. 'I've got one last piece of business planned for him this evening, and

that should be that. I think we'll be finished with
him then.'

'You'll let him come home?' asked Jack.

'I'm sure of it,' said the doctor. 'But the test I'm
planning for today is going to leave him feeling a
little bit groggy. It might be just as well if you tell
everyone not to bother visiting him this evening.
Especially as he'll probably be discharged first thing
tomorrow.'

'Great!' said Jack. 'That's brilliant. I'll tell Mum
and Dad.'

Jack stared at the doctor's lined and weathered
face. For some reason alarm bells were ringing in
his head.

'Did you know that this hospital used to be the
pest house in the old days?' he said to the doctor.
'You know? The plague house?' He had no idea why
he was telling the doctor that. He just knew he had
to.

The doctor nodded. 'As a matter of fact, I did,'
he said. 'My family have been doctors in this town
for generations.' A ragged smile cracked across his
face. 'Believe it or not, I can trace my ancestry all
the way back to Stuart times! Right back to the reign
of Charles II.' He looked up at the three friends. 'I
have to go now. It's been nice speaking with you.'
The window began its smooth upward glide.
'Remember – no visitors for Tom tonight.'

'Yes. Got it.'

Light reflected off the glass.

'Cheerio,' said the doctor. 'I'll see you tomorrow,
maybe.'

He gave a brief wave. The car glided off.

Jack stood staring after it, disquiet trembling like

a trapped butterfly under his ribs. King Charles II had reigned at the time of the Great Plague.

'You know something,' said Regan, her voice breaking into Jack's blurry thoughts. 'That guy reminds me of someone. I just can't think who.'

CHAPTER THIRTEEN
Lord Have Mercy
On Us All

It was no more than a twenty-minute walk from the hospital to Wakes Lane, where Regan lived in her large, detached house, in a wide avenue full of large, detached houses. Bell Green. The most exclusive district in the whole of Lychford. The Vanderlindens wouldn't have considered anything else. Once there, the three friends would finally have the peace and solitude to discuss the afternoon's events.

Between the hospital and the Lane lay a slightly run-down area of second-hand shops and soulless, grey, neglected houses.

The three friends walked through these depressing backstreets in silence, their spirits weighed down by a dull misery that seemed to come seeping up out of the ground. Maybe it was just the airless heat of that relentless summer. Maybe the loveless decay of the place.

In the long-ago summer of 1665, Lychford had been pinned down under a sun just as severe and unforgiving.

A dry wind stirred the rubbish and the dust in the

streets. A sheet of newspaper flapped by in the wind, looking for all the world like some crooked, deformed bird.

Damp, baking-hot, soap-sour air billowed out from a launderette. Regan glanced at the grimy window. Information had been roughly lettered on the glass in red paint.

Two garments for the price of one. Special rates for duvets. Service wash available.

Dust blew into Regan's eyes. The painted message melted and re-moulded itself.

Lord Have Mercy On Us All.

She stared at the red, glistening words. The letters dribbled blood down the glass.

'Uh . . . guys . . .?' she croaked, grabbing at Frankie's sleeve. 'Do you wanna take a look at this?'

Frankie and Jack looked.

'What?' Jack asked.

'Can't you *see?*'

'No. What?' Jack said. 'What are we supposed to be looking at?'

Frankie hooked her hand under Regan's arm and towed her away from the shopfront.

Frankie's voice was tight and pinched. 'Don't look,' she said. 'Pay no attention.'

Regan squirmed, her head wrenching over her shoulder. 'But . . .'

'Don't look!' Frankie hissed. 'Don't think about it. Ignore it.'

'Can you see what it says?' asked Regan.

'Yes. No. *Yes.*'

'I don't see anything,' said Jack.

'You're darned lucky, then!' said Regan. She

stared at Frankie. 'It's real, isn't it? It's really there. It's not just in my head.'

'I don't know,' said Frankie. 'I just want to get out of here.' She lifted her head and sniffed. 'The air. Can you smell it?'

Regan sniffed. She had expected to smell vinegar, but instead she caught a whiff of something else. 'It's like down in that cellar,' she said. 'When the wall collapsed.'

'Worse,' said Frankie. 'And it's getting stronger, too.'

Jack stood tense in the middle of the pavement. He was sensing nothing. He saw nothing. He smelled nothing.

Doom!

The air shivered and for a moment the sun seemed to tremble on the stretched sheet of the sky. Frankie twisted her head to look back at Jack, her eyes filled with horror.

'I heard it,' said Jack. 'Something's happening.'

'Let's get out of here,' said Regan.

Doom!

The bell tolled, its doleful resonance rolling out over the rooftops like death giving voice.

They heard a cry. It came from a narrow alley between two shops. A dark figure stumbled out of the slot and crumpled on the pavement.

A man. In a navy blue suit.

They ran to him. They helped him as he struggled to sit up. He groaned. He leaned back against the wall. He was wearing a white shirt and a blue-striped tie. His glasses hung askew across his sweating face. His hair stuck to his forehead. His face was disfigured with red weals. He coughed weakly.

'Help! For God's sake help us!' A young voice. A woman's voice. Calling from the far side of the street. Frankie turned, her head spinning.

The young woman hung out of an upstairs window. She had a punk haircut. She was wearing a T-shirt. Her arms stretched down, her mouth was wide open, distorted with fear. Her skin was livid with red blotches.

Beneath her, the door to the house was painted with a red cross.

Suddenly the street was full of people, wandering aimlessly, staggering, arms outstretched, slipping and falling, tumbling over one another as though playing some grotesque game of blind-man's bluff.

But they weren't people dredged up out of the baleful past – they were dressed in modern-day clothes. They were just people – ordinary people, their faces destroyed by the plague welts, skin purple, eyes sunken and black-rimmed, cheeks hollow, lips trailing bloody saliva.

They moaned as they stumbled and reeled. They cried out as they fell and were trampled. And they gave off a choking stench.

Jack staggered back, gagging at the stink.

Ring a ring o' roses, a pocket full of posies,
Atishoo! Atishoo! We all fall down!

Regan watched in dread as a line of children, dancing hand in hand, wound their way through the milling throng. Their voices were shrill and joyless, their faces ruinous with the livid red rash of the plague.

'Run!' Jack yelled.

A disfigured, long-haired, blotch-faced man in denims stood in front of Frankie. He beckoned, as though hoping to draw her into the macabre dance.

Jack grabbed her and hauled her away. She seemed to come out of a dream. They ran. Regan was with them.

The hideous crowd jostled them and blocked their way, but they ploughed on, careless of the screams and shouts that echoed around their ears.

'Not real! Not real!' Frankie panted as they ran. 'You're not real!'

And then the plague-ridden mob was gone.

The street was empty.

A wing of newspaper flapped by in the dusty wind, skimming low over the road.

'If you don't believe in them, they can't exist!' Jack gasped. He looked at the two girls. 'You've got to remember that!'

Doom!

The bell gave out its desolate toll.

Regan gave Jack a sideways look. 'And that?' she said.

'It's in our heads,' said Jack. 'It can't hurt us.'

'Sez you!' muttered Regan. She looked at her two friends. She gave them a feeble grin. 'Race you guys home?'

Wheels rattled. Hooves clattered on a hard surface. A harness jingled. Leather cracked and creaked. A whip spat.

A black coach came hurtling around the corner, drawn by two black horses at a frenzied gallop. Their eyes were wild; spittle foamed at their mouths. The driver sat high, lagged in a huge black cloak. A hat was drawn down, shadowing his face. His whip-arm rose and fell.

As it turned the corner, two wheels lifted. For a moment the carriage was balanced on two rims. Then it came crashing down again. The windows were hung with flapping black curtains.

The horses veered and charged towards the three friends. The black coach bounced, threatening to tip the driver from his precarious perch.

Frankie reacted first. She threw herself sideways, grabbing Jack and pulling him along with her. Jack tried to snatch hold of Regan, but he was too late.

She only had a moment. She froze. The horses bore down on her. The noise was tumultuous.

'Regan!' Frankie screamed.

Regan flung her arms across her face.

The coach and horses rode straight through her and blasted itself out of existence at her back.

Regan opened an eye. She was unharmed. Untouched. Flabbergasted.

'*Unreal* . . .' She looked at her friends. 'I'm never gonna get used to this,' she said. And then her legs gave way and she found herself sitting in the road.

They helped her up.

'Come on,' said Frankie. 'We're almost there now.' She pointed to where a road forked off to the right. 'It's down there, isn't it?'

Regan nodded. Down the length of that road, across another, through a skinny little alley, and then they'd be only a minute away from Wakes Lane. And safety. They hoped.

They came to the end of the first street without anything else happening to them. The desolate bell was silent. They began to hope that maybe the terror had run its course.

They crossed the road. They saw maybe half a dozen people. A woman pushing a pram. A couple of old ladies chatting on a corner. A man posting a letter in a pillar box. A girl on a bike. Normality.

Frankie was the first to hear the sound. It was just as they came to the mouth of the alley. A faint, sharp sound, like distant fingernails rattling on metal. Or like surf on shingle.

The alley wound its way between rearing brick walls.

Frankie looked around, trying to pinpoint the indistinct noise.

'What?' Jack asked.

'Nothing . . .' murmured Frankie. 'I don't think . . .'

They walked quickly through the alley. Brick gave way to tall wooden fencing. Bushes hung trailing leaf-laden arms over the fence-tops. Creeping convolvulus forced planks apart. White, bell-shaped flowers hung limp in the heat. Weeds sprouted between cracked paving stones. Nettles massed. The fences tottered, deep in decay. Through missing and rotting boards, an overgrown wasteland could be glimpsed.

The sound grew.

Regan looked around. 'What's that?'

'I don't know,' said Frankie. 'I've been hearing it for a while.'

Scrabbling. A steadily growing noise of scrabbling.

And another noise. A rushing, hissing sound, sibilant and somehow disturbing.

The noise seemed to be coming from all around

them. They stopped, staring about them as the noise grew and grew.

'What *is* that?' breathed Regan.

They were in a bend of the alley, unable to see any more than a few metres in either direction.

The noise was like rushing water. No. Not water. But . . . something . . .

Something racing towards them in a commotion of scratching and chittering and jostling.

The three friends shrank together.

A black tide.

Jack saw it in his head a split second before it burst upon them. A turmoil of black bodies. A confusion of small black shapes. Lean, ravenous creatures trailing naked tails. Bead-bright eyes glittered. Needle teeth. Hooked claws.

'This isn't real!' Jack shouted above the clamour.

Frankie screamed.

The rats erupted all around them, pouring over the wooden fences, surging in through the holes, boiling along the alley in an evil flood.

'Not real!' yelled Regan.

A writhing mass of rats, tangled like a ball of worms, came boiling over the fence above her. They dropped like a squealing rabble of evil fruit.

She drew back. 'You're not real!'

A rat flew at her face. She struck out at the screeching thing. Blood-drop eyes glittered. Sharp teeth snapped.

'Ow!' Regan recoiled, almost tripping over the seething carpet of creatures. There were white scores down the back of her hand. Teeth-marks. She stared in disbelief. Blood welled.

The rats were real.

CHAPTER FOURTEEN
Rats

One section of the high fencing was bare of the horde of skriking and scratching rats. Jack hurled himself at it. It was their only hope. A shoulder-charge against the rotting wood sent the planks flying into splinters.

Jack found himself sprawling in a cradle of spiked and barbed branches, woodchips whizzing around his ears. The fence had virtually disintegrated under his onslaught. He dragged himself to his feet, fighting loose of the clawing thorns.

Nothing needed to be said. The two girls were hard on his heels, clambering over the ruins of the fence. Regan was sucking her hand. The rats were all around them.

Jack forged a path through the knee-high tangle of undergrowth. He had no time to chose a direction. There was only one thought in his head: to get away from those rats. Those hundreds of vicious black rats.

The two girls waded in his wake. Pliant limbs of underbrush dragged at their legs. Tough grasses

wound around ankles. Thorns gouged and
scratched. Powder-dry pollen rose in clouds, clinging
to their sweating faces as they ploughed on.

Jack was aware of a slight incline. He looked up.
There were houses. A barrier of black iron railings.
All around him he could hear a frantic rustling. All
around them the grasses were on the move. He saw
the occasional hump of a sleek black back through
the foliage. The rats were keeping up with them.

Regan glanced around. The cleft in the undergrowth opened by their flight was filled with rats.

They came to the railings. Chest height. Not an
impossible climb, but not easy either. They were all
breathless.

Frankie didn't hesitate. She launched herself at
the railings. She balanced on both hands, bringing
her legs swinging up and over. She landed on the
other side.

Jack dragged himself over and fell, cracking his
elbow and knee on the paving stones.

Regan was shorter than her two friends. She
grabbed at the top rail and strained. She heaved up.
The top rail bit into her stomach. She lost grip and
fell back. She curled up in a ball, expecting the rats
to swarm all over her.

'Regan! Come *on*!'

Frankie's voice. Regan lifted her head. The rats
were all around her. But they weren't attacking.
Regan stood up, cringing back against the railings.

A thousand twinkling eyes watched her.

She turned and climbed, helped by Jack and
Frankie.

As soon as Regan was over the railings, the rats
began to move again. They surged out through the

railings and surrounded the three friends in a black sea.

But there was an intelligence behind those blood-shot eyes.

'Oh my gosh!' murmured Frankie. 'Do you *see*?'

The blanket of rats opened in one direction, leaving a narrow clear trail, wide enough for the three friends to walk single file.

A road ran alongside the railings. There were run-down houses. Smashed street-lamps. Abandoned cars. Wind-swept banks of litter. A junk yard breeding rust.

No people.

'I guess we don't have much choice,' muttered Regan. She nudged past Jack and began to walk the path left for them by the rats.

Frankie and Jack looked at one another. Regan was right: what other choice did they have? The rats had already shown themselves capable of inflicting injury. Regan was still sucking at her bleeding hand.

They walked slowly. The rats kept up with them, a moving mantle of malign watchfulness.

They were steered into the junk yard. They were led through piles of corroded metal. There was a wire fence. A section was torn away. The rats guided them to the gap. There was a stony alley. Walls of ugly yellow brick. A road. Deserted. Another back way.

Somehow the rats seemed to know exactly how to drive the three friends through the deserted, hidden arteries of the old town. But where were they being taken?

Jack tried to think.

The sun was fierce in the sky. Lower than Jack

would have expected. Glaring in their eyes. That meant they were being driven west. He tried to imagine a map of the town. West? Where would that take them? It was no good – he didn't know the town anything like well enough to be able to guess where they were heading.

'Know something, guys?' whispered Regan.

'What?' Frankie's head was throbbing with the strain of their enforced march. She had tried to step away from the narrow pathway, but the rats had clotted together to stop her. She had a bad feeling about what might happen if they tried to break free. Three of them. A couple of thousand rats. Bad.

'I don't know about you,' said Regan, 'but I think we're nuts to keep letting these darned *rodents* run this show.' She glanced around at her friends. 'I mean, get real, guys – these critters aren't exactly gonna be taking us for a picnic. You know?' She lowered her voice, as if she believed the rats might overhear and understand. 'We gotta break clear, huh?'

Jack had come to the same conclusion. 'Frankie? You know Lychford better than either of us. Can you work out where we're being taken?'

Frankie frowned. Her mind had been filled with the despair of the moment: she'd given no thought to their ultimate destination.

She tried to concentrate.

It was difficult to work out how long they had been herded along by the swarming creatures. Minutes? Hours? The sun was skimming the rooftops. It felt to Frankie as if they'd been walking this malevolent trail for ever; as if the rats had always been there. As if they would always be there.

'I think . . .' She struggled. 'I think we're heading towards . . .' Her voice died. The truth of their peril had hit her like a bolt of lightning. 'Oh my gosh! I know where they're taking us.' She grabbed Regan's arm. 'Stop! Stop right now!'

'Where? What?'

'We're only a few streets away from Marlowe Road,' said Frankie.

Regan blinked at her. 'Uh . . . I don't think . . .'

'The factory is in Marlowe Road,' hissed Frankie. 'The factory where they're doing the dig! Don't you get it? We're being taken back to the plague pit.'

Regan made a sound like escaping steam.

'This has to stop *now*,' said Jack. 'We have to break free before it's too late.'

Regan turned to face them. The rats knitted in tighter around their feet – leaving just the one route. West. Towards the pit, and whatever nightmare waited there for them.

'OK, guys,' she said slowly. 'This is the moment when one of us has to say, hey, I have a foolproof plan to get us out of here.' There was an uneasy silence. 'Uh-huh,' said Regan. 'I . . . see . . .'

'Wait,' Frankie said. 'It's not a plan, exactly, it's just a thought. Maybe if we can just get out to where people are? We haven't seen a single person since before the alley. If we can get out into a main street, maybe . . .' She stared in fear and disgust at the rats. 'Maybe we'll be able to lose them.'

'So,' said Regan. 'We just make a run for it, right? And hope we hit a populated area before . . . uh . . . before . . .' She didn't need to finish the sentence. Before the rats got them. She looked around. 'Which way?'

They were in another back alley, hemmed by brick walls.

'I . . . I think we want to go that way,' said Frankie. She indicated the right-hand wall of the alley. 'If I've got it right, those houses we can see run down one side of Juniper Street. There are shops and all-sorts along there. There's bound to be people.'

'Sounds good,' said Regan. 'Even if the rats follow us, we'll have back-up to beat them off.'

The rats began to stir impatiently around their feet. Beady eyes peered up at them. A claw scratched at Frankie's shoe. An insistent screeching began to build, a noise that scraped at the inside of their skulls like nails down a blackboard.

Jack pointed to a door set into the wall, a little way ahead of them. The long wall was punctuated by several such doors. Jack assumed they must lead into backyards or gardens. He could see that the tall houses beyond were set slightly apart. Side alleys. Alleys that should lead out to the street.

'That way?' he said.

The girls nodded.

'Let me lead,' Jack said to Regan. 'I'm stronger. The door might be bolted.'

'You might be stronger, man,' said Regan, 'but you sure ain't any more determined. I'll go first, if it's all the same to you.'

The rats began to clamour. Needle teeth tore at the hem of Regan's jeans. There was a renewed urgency in the churning of the loathsome animals. They were nearing the end of their long journey. Soon it would all be over.

'OK, OK,' hissed Regan. 'Keep your fur on! I'm going. I'm going!'

As soon as Regan started to walk, the rats seemed to calm down a little. They swept alongside the three of them, chittering softly to themselves, their claws pattering sharply. The rustle of their lean bodies was a sound to make the skin crawl.

Regan tried to blank her mind out. It was pointless to allow herself to imagine what might happen when they made their break. A person could go nuts!

They neared the door.

'OK,' Regan whispered determinedly. 'It's show time!'

She took in a deep breath. She launched herself at the door with all her strength. The door cracked, giving slightly as she was sprung back from it. The rats let out a wild multi-voiced screech and boiled up around the three friends like a storm-tossed ocean of black water.

She hurled herself forward a second time, the rats foaming at her legs.

She was bounced back.

The door stood firm.

CHAPTER FIFTEEN

Past Poisons Present

An enormous uproar burst from beyond the door.

Dogs barking.

The frenzied barking of a whole pack of dogs.

Regan hardly had time to register the startling noise before she was swept up from behind and found herself heading breathlessly for another collision with the door.

Frankie and Jack had acted simultaneously. Regan couldn't break the door. That was obvious. More weight was needed. The rats were massing to attack. The two friends caught Regan up in their charge.

The door burst open with a wrench of breaking wood.

The three of them pitched into the walled backyard. It was long and narrow. All down one side stood wooden enclosures, linked together. Behind chicken-wire, a dozen or more dogs were barking frantically and throwing themselves at the wire. Big dogs. Black and dark brown – like Rottweilers, with blazing eyes and slavering jaws. It was some kind of kennels. The bedlam of noise was deafening.

Jack glanced back to check his friends were all right, then he sped towards the thin alleyway that run up the side of the house.

Frankie was only a step behind him. She jumped bags of feed. The dogs were going crazy, hurling themselves at the chicken-wire, raking with their claws, maddened by the instinct to set upon the rats; the multitude of rats that were already pouring in through the open doorway.

Regan stumbled and nearly fell. She kicked out and a skreeling black shape was sent spinning. Score one for the good guys!

For a fleeting instant the leading rats hesitated at the sight and sound of their age-old canine enemies. But those still in the alley pushed forwards. The torrent could not be arrested for long.

Regan glimpsed a face at an upstairs window of the house. Angry. Shouting, arms gesticulating. The man was looking down at them: at Regan and Frankie and Jack. He banged on the window. Angry. He didn't even seem to register the rats that spilled into his backyard.

Jack reached the gate at the far end of the alleyway. He jerked the bolt free and dragged the gate wide. It opened onto a busy street. Cars. People. Shops. All the normal, blissful confusion of a main street. A bus was parked across the other side of the road.

Jack blundered out onto the pavement.

'Oi – watch it!'

'Sorry. Sorry.'

'Kids!'

Jack ran across the road. Frankie was just behind him. Car horns blared.

'Stupid kids!'

Regan followed. She flicked an eye over her shoulder. The alley was a seething crush of black bodies.

Jack rounded the front of the bus. The driver stared down at him. The doors hissed closed. Jack skidded around onto the pavement. He banged on the narrow glass door-panels with both hands.

The driver shook his head.

He was behind schedule as it was. He didn't have time to be messed about by stupid kids. It was always the same. Some smart-alecky kid would come charging up the moment you closed the doors. It was like some sort of idiotic game they played.

Frankie hit the doors, shouting and banging on the glass alongside Jack.

'Let us on! Please!'

The rats were pouring out of the alleyway.

No one seemed to notice them. Regan had expected people to scream and run – but they seemed oblivious of the tide of horrible creatures that surged around their feet.

With a great show of irritation and reluctance, the driver opened the doors.

The three friends threw themselves on board.

'One at a time! One at a time!'

The doors wheezed closed. Regan pulled her foot away. A writhing rat was trapped halfway through the door, held in the hard rubber jaws. More rats threw themselves at the glass. There was a sickening noise as the door squeezed shut and the trapped rat was killed.

The rats massed around the bus.

No one could see them.

It was as though two separate pictures – two separate realities – had become superimposed one over the other. In one, people were going about their everyday business; in the other, the pavements, the road, the entire street was swarming with rats.

Jack slapped some money down. 'Three . . . to . . . Bell . . . Green . . .' he gasped.

It was impossible. The rats were hurling themselves at the bus. The three friends could hear the thudding of their bodies, like a kind of evil hail.

'Any monkey business and you're off,' said the driver. He had the three friends down as troublemakers. He wasn't having any nonsense on his bus.

Jack led the girls to the back of the bus. A few people looked at them without much interest. Outside the rats were screeching and scrabbling at the vehicle, desperate to get at them.

The bus shuddered into movement.

The friends threw themselves onto the long back seat. As the bus accelerated, they saw the rats running.

They looked at one another. Nothing needed to be said. It was obvious that they were the only people who could see the calamitous army of black rats.

Gradually, as the bus gathered speed, the filthy, swarming throng was left behind.

Regan sank into her seat, throwing her arms over her head.

Her voice was an exhausted mumble. 'Wake me up when we hit reality, guys!'

They were in the bathroom at Regan's house. Frankie and Jack had never been to the huge house before. Regan was not too hot on inviting people home. It was a little too much like showing off. Welcome, poor people, to the Vanderlinden Mansion.

The bathroom was the size of a normal living room. Regan was sitting on the side of the bath while Frankie smoothed a sticking-plaster onto the back of her hand. The shallow wounds were stinging a little from some antiseptic ointment that Frankie had spread over them.

'There you go,' said Frankie. 'But don't leave it, if it starts to hurt or swell up or anything. It might be infected.'

They checked for other bites or scratches. The rats had done them little physical damage. Clawed shoes mostly. One leg of Regan's jeans was shredded at the hem.

'Designer jeans,' she sighed, looking at the damage. 'Five hundred dollars a pair. Rats!' She gave a sickly grin. 'Rats? Geddit?'

Jack was at the little window that looked down onto the deep driveway with its raked gravel and its well-tended rose bushes. He held the curtain aside and watched the road beyond the high privet hedge. His head was full of danger, but he couldn't tell whether it was just an echo of their ordeal or an omen of something yet to come.

Jennie was nowhere to be seen.

Fixing Regan up had been their first priority once they were behind closed doors.

They had been surprised to see the time. It was early evening. Hours had passed since they had left the hospital. They'd been in some terrible half-world where time and distance meant nothing.

Frankie washed her hands at the basin. She hooked her hair behind her ear and looked at the others. 'You know, I didn't recognize half the places those ... things took us to. Some of it was like Lychford ... but other places were ...' she shrugged. 'I don't know. Not Lychford. Not the Lychford I know, anyway.'

'Let's go somewhere more comfortable,' said Regan. 'I'd like to be sitting down before we get into exactly what the heck is going on.' She gave a weak grin. 'It'll save me falling flat on my face again!'

She led them down to a sumptuously furnished reception room.

'Ignore the fixtures and fittings,' Regan said as she plumped down in an armchair. 'It all came with the house.' She hooked a leg over the arm. Jack and Frankie sat in a padded Chesterfield couch.

There was an uncomfortable silence.

'No one else saw the rats,' Frankie said eventually. 'But one of them bit Regan. I felt them around my ankles. They were real.'

'Real to us,' said Jack.

'And what exactly does that mean?' Regan asked. 'If a thing's real, it's real, right?'

Jack looked at her. 'Is it?'

She closed her eyes. 'OK!' she said, cutting her hands through the air. 'Time out!' She stared at Jack. 'What are you trying to say, man? That reality is in the eye of the beholder, or something?'

Jack nodded. 'Maybe it is,' he said. 'Maybe that's exactly what we're caught up with here. Different realities, sort of ... hitting together. Or maybe it's us. Maybe we've got trapped between realities. One foot here, and one foot . . . I don't know . . . in the seventeenth century.'

'Well, that makes a whole lot of sense,' said Regan. 'Not!'

'Something horrible was let loose when the plague pit collapsed,' Frankie said quietly. 'And it seems to be getting stronger all the time. At first it was just that bell . . . and the stuff that Regan was smelling. But now . . .' She stared at the tall velvet-draped window. 'What next? I mean, what's out there?' She trembled. 'How are we ever going to get out of this in one piece? And where can we go? How do we stop it all?'

'We need help,' said Jack. He looked at Regan. 'Remember what you said before? About Tom being the real victim, and about us just suffering from the fallout?'

'Yeah. Sure. So?'

'So, that means Tom is the key,' said Jack. 'Or, at least, Will Hilliard is. Tom let his . . . his consciousness . . . out of the pit when he kicked the wall in. And that consciousness is very angry.'

'Tell me about it,' said Regan. 'I guess I'd be a little ticked off if my entire family had been wiped out by some maniac doctor-guy just so he could squeeze a few bucks out of our belongings.' She frowned. 'You think all this craziness is being caused by Will? Because he's angry about what happened?'

'I think Will is at the centre of it,' said Jack. 'But I'm really worried that there's something else going on as well.'

'Like what?' asked Frankie.

'I'm not sure. But . . . but it's got something to do

with Dr Bludworth.' Jack shivered. 'I can feel him. He's out there. Somewhere.'

'Wonderful,' groaned Regan. 'As if the rats weren't enough, there's a mad, dead poisoner on the loose.'

'There's more,' said Jack. 'Dr Fairfax said that his family have been doctors in Lychford going all the way back to Stuart times.'

'OK.' Frankie's grey eyes were fixed on Jack's face. 'And King Charles II was on the throne at the time of the Great Plague – and he was a Stuart king. With you so far. Carry on.'

'Dr Bludworth gave Will's family poison to drink,' Jack said hesitantly. He was trying to order his thoughts as he spoke. 'Remember how Tom reacted when Dr Fairfax tried to give him that drink of water?'

'He went *postal*!' said Regan. 'He flipped out!'

'Exactly,' said Jack. 'And we all thought it was because Tom was out of his head. But what if there was another reason?'

'Such as what?' Frankie asked.

'Think about this,' said Jack. 'Tom is Will, right? And because we were there when Will was let out, we've been caught up in all this stuff. We've been . . . *infected*, yeah? But . . . well . . . suppose this stuff could infect other people, too? Even people who weren't there?'

'You mean, like the direct descendant of the man who murdered the Hilliards,' breathed Frankie. 'That's what you're saying, isn't it? You think Dr Fairfax is a great-great-great-something-or-other of Bludworth. You think he's been infected, too. Infected by Bludworth.'

'I don't see it,' said Regan. 'What's he ever done to make you figure that?' She sat bolt upright, slamming her hand over her mouth. '*Ohmigosh!* Jack, it just clicked! His face. Fairfax's face! He looks just how Tom . . . Will, I mean – he looks just the way Will described Bludworth!' She slumped back. 'No. Wait. Wait. That doesn't prove anything. It could just be a coincidence.'

'Maybe,' said Jack. 'But what if it isn't? What if the appearance of Will's consciousness inside Tom has triggered something in Dr Fairfax? He told me that he would finish with Tom this evening. And he said to tell everyone not to visit until tomorrow.'

'Meaning, he's got something planned for tonight,' said Frankie. 'Something bad for Tom. But why would he want to harm him? The poisoning and all that miserable stuff was over and done with centuries ago. It doesn't make sense.'

'You don't get it, do you?' Jack said, staring at her with troubled eyes. 'It doesn't need to make *sense*. There doesn't have to be a *purpose* behind any of this.' He looked from Frankie to Regan. 'Don't you see? There doesn't need to be a reason. The plague didn't need a reason. There was no point behind it. It just *happened*.' His thoughts had become clear at last. The confusion was finally lifted. 'The plague infected thousands of people. It killed them. And Bludworth has infected Dr Fairfax – taken him over – and he's going to kill Tom! He's going to kill Tom tonight!'

CHAPTER SIXTEEN
Under Siege

It was several seconds before anyone felt able to respond to Jack's words. Not that they doubted him for a moment. The conviction in his eyes was enough to dispel any doubt.

'We need help,' Frankie murmured. 'We can't deal with this on our own.'

Regan stood up. She walked over to an antique side-table and picked the telephone up in both hands. She placed it in Frankie's lap.

'There you go,' she said expressionlessly. 'Call someone who'll believe us.'

Frankie stared down at the phone. Regan was right. Who'd believe them?

'Darryl would believe us,' Jack said. 'At least, he'd try to.'

'He doesn't have a phone,' said Regan. 'He lives halfway across town.' She looked out of the window at the gathering twilight. 'Anyone feel like volunteering to go over there?' It was just one of Darryl's eccentricities that he had a line for his modem, but no actual telephone. Darryl wasn't a great one for talking to people direct.

The friends may have been fooling themselves, but the house felt like a sanctuary – a small haven of sanity in all the chaos that was fomenting out there in the growing night. None of them wanted to risk the rats again, or whatever else might come crawling out of the darkness now that the day was dying.

'Rhea!' Frankie exclaimed. 'Rhea's got a phone. We could call her.' She swiped up the receiver and tapped out a series of numbers. Frankie was good with numbers. They stuck to her brain like jam to a blanket. And she'd been the one asked by Darryl to call Rhea and arrange a time and date for their visit to the dig in Marlowe Road.

'What are you going to tell her?' asked Jack.

'I dunno,' Frankie said. 'I'll think of something. It's ringing.' She crossed her fingers. 'Please be there. Pleasepleasepleasepleasepleasepleasepleaseplease . . .'

There was the sound of the phone being picked up. And a familiar young woman's voice.

'Hello?'

'Rhea?'

'Yes.'

'It's Frankie. Frankie Fitzgerald.'

'Oh, hello Frankie. Has something happened?'

Frankie felt quite blown away by that question. What on earth do you say after a day like they'd just had? Battalions of rats. Clashing realities. Ancient enmities come alive again. Tom in deadly peril. *He-e-e-elp!*

'Um . . . it's . . . you see . . .' *I'll think of something.* 'We . . . we need to get in touch with Darryl really,

really urgently. But he hasn't got a phone. I know it's a terrible cheek, but we were wondering if you could . . . um . . . drive over to his place and give him a message from us. *It's very important.* Honest.' She felt like adding: *It's a matter of life and death,* but that would just sound too over the top. Like a joke.

'Where are you?' Rhea's voice took on a sharp edge. 'What's happened?'

'It's . . . complicated,' said Frankie. She gave Jack and Regan an anxious look. Was Rhea going to demand explanations? Was she going to come over all adult and just add to their problems? 'Something's happened. We need Darryl's help. I really don't know what else I can tell you right now.'

'OK, OK,' came the voice down the phone. 'You don't have to spell it out. I can be at Darryl's place in . . . ten minutes. What do you want me to tell him?'

Frankie let out a breath of relief. 'Oh, thanks, Rhea. Really. Thanks. Just tell him we're all at Regan's. It's urgent and we need him to take us to the hospital.'

Rhea's voice cut across her. 'Has something happened to Tom?'

'Well, no,' Frankie admitted. 'We don't think so. Not yet. But something might. We need to get Tom out of the hospital as soon as possible—'

Jack was scissoring his arms through the air and mouthing: *No! Don't tell her that!* No way would Rhea understand why they needed to hijack Tom from his hospital bed.

Frankie shot Jack an apologetic look. Big mouth!

'OK, Frankie, leave it with me,' said Rhea. 'Just

stay put. Darryl should be with you in . . . say . . . half an hour at most. OK?'

'Brilliant! You don't realize how much—'

'It's fine, Frankie. Don't worry. I'm leaving right now.'

Frankie put the receiver down. She sank back on the couch, her face split with a relieved smile. 'Phew!'

'She went for it?' said Regan. 'Even after that crack about getting Tom out of the hospital?'

'Yes. She went for it. She said half an hour.'

Regan sat heavily on the broad arm of the couch. She folded her arms.

'Uh . . . Jack? I guess you have some cunning plan worked out for exactly what we do once we've gotten Tom clear of Dr Fairfax . . . or Bludworth . . . or whoever the heck the guy is right now? I mean, you do know what happens next, huh?'

Jack looked at her. 'Yes,' he said. 'I do. We need to get Will Hilliard out of Tom.'

Frankie's eyes turned questioningly to him.

'Uh-huh?' Regan cocked her head. 'And how do we do that, exactly?'

'Exactly?'

'Yeah.'

Jack shook his head. 'I haven't got the faintest idea.'

Regan opened her mouth. She closed it again without speaking.

Doom!

Softly, on the edge of hearing, a distant, forsaken bell began slowly to toll.

Frankie stood at the window, staring out into the evening. The sky was sultry, still lambent with a deep-water blue, like a turquoise cinema curtain lit from beneath. The odd star twinkled. A grim glitter. It reminded her of the light in a rat's eye.

The lethargic bell whispered on the mind's horizon. A sound so low that a spoken word blotted it out. The trouble was that no one felt like talking. The quiet bell held everyone's attention, like the pulse of some lurking monster that grew stronger as daylight ebbed away.

The euphoria of Darryl's expected arrival had quickly evaporated.

Regan had suggested closing the curtains, but Frankie hated the idea. If something was skulking out there, she wanted to see it. The bulky privet hedge closed off most of the view at the end of the drive. Occasionally people walked past the gateway – twenty metres away. Cars swept by. The shadows under the bushes and walls deepened and grew, holes in the world that expanded moment by moment. They sent out tributaries of concealment, welling out over the world, joining and spreading until there was more darkness than light.

Frankie stared into these eclipses until her eyes ached.

Something was out there. They all felt it.

Jack sat bent over on the couch, his head in his hands. Warnings of danger were going off in his head like blood-red fireworks. If he closed his eyes, all he could see was pulsating redness. And a wrongness. A terrible *wrongness*.

Regan was pacing up and down the long room like a stir-crazy tiger. At every turn she looked at her watch.

Where was Darryl?

They all longed for the clunky, clattery sound of his dilapidated old grey van. It was his only source of income, that van. He worked as a kind of odd-job man, running little errands around Lychford: delivering stuff and ferrying things about. Not much of a living, but it paid his rent and fed him and covered the cost of the electricity that his computer gobbled up.

Where was he?

Frankie stiffened.

She heard distant laughter. High-pitched, humourless laughter that wound up into a wailing scream and was cut off.

Jack lifted his head and stared out of the window. Regan had stopped in her tracks. They had all heard it.

A cloud of darkness glided out of shadow. It slid slowly across the width of the driveway.

Two people carrying a coffin on their shoulders. A bent figure walked behind. Sobbing.

Frankie heard the deliberate *clop, clop, clop, clop* of heavy hooves.

Something hit the window. Frankie let out a scream and jerked back from the terrible, hideous apparition. It was an emaciated baby, pushed against the glass by a plague-ravaged woman. A dead baby. The grief in the woman's eyes was shattering. Heart-rending.

The woman clutched the dead infant back to her chest. Her blood-daubed hand beat at the window and she wailed in anguish.

And then they were gone: mother and baby together. But bloody smears were left on the glass.

Jack stood up, his legs trembling.

Frankie was in a heap on the carpet, her head tucked in under her arms.

Jack crouched by her side. He touched her shoulder. She convulsed away from him. He couldn't think of anything comforting to say.

She looked up at him. 'It's OK . . .' she murmured.

Regan stood just behind them. 'It is?' she breathed. 'You could have fooled me.'

A new sound. A car. It stopped beyond the drive, hidden by the hedge.

Frankie lifted her head. 'Darryl?'

'It doesn't sound right,' said Jack. They heard a car door open and close. A dark figure moved to the gate. Opened it. Not Darryl – in silhouette, Darryl looked like a half-starved stork. This person was short and stocky.

The figure vanished again. The car door opened and closed. The car came nosing in through the gate. Tyres crunched gravel. The car came slowly up to the house. Security lights blazed on, throwing pools of light out over the approaching car.

'It's Rhea!' exclaimed Regan.

Frankie scrambled up. 'Is Darryl with her?'

'No. I don't think so.'

They ran to the front door. Rhea was already standing there.

'Darryl wasn't in,' she said. 'His landlady didn't know when he'd be back.' She looked from face to face. 'You sounded like you needed help really badly. Can I do anything?'

'We think Dr Fairfax is going to kill Tom!' Regan blurted. 'We have to get him out of that hospital.'

'Regan!' Jack was horrified. Rhea wouldn't

understand. He looked at the young woman. 'It's really difficult to explain,' he said.

Rhea lifted her hands. 'Then don't try,' she said. 'Darryl told me you were good people. If Darryl trusts you, then so can I.' She indicated the waiting car. 'Coming?'

'You bet!' said Regan.

The three friends ran to the car. At every crunching step Frankie expected something to grab her ankles and pull her down. They jumped in and slammed the doors. Frankie up front, Regan and Jack in the back. Jack flicked the internal locks on.

He couldn't believe Rhea was showing so much faith in them. Anyone else would have wanted at least *some* explanation.

'The hospital? Right?' said Rhea.

'Yes!' said Jack.

The wheels spat gravel as Rhea guided the car out onto the road. The three friends were pushed back in the seats as Rhea put her foot down. The car sped off.

Frankie stared out of the windows, expecting to see some manifestation of separate realities merging again. But there was nothing. The noise of the car engine drowned out the plague bell and the streets of Lychford held no visible horrors.

'I assume you don't want anyone to know what you're doing,' Rhea said as the car swept along. 'When you take Tom, I mean?'

'We don't want Bludworth to know, that's for sure!' said Regan.

'Bludworth?'

'She means Dr Fairfax,' said Jack. 'If I'm right, he's going to try to hurt Tom tonight.' He tried to make the half-explanation sound convincing. 'We just need to get Tom away until we can work out what to do next.'

'OK,' said Rhea. 'Here's what we're going to do. I'll go in the main way, and I'll ask to speak to . . . what's-his-name . . . Fairfax. And while I keep him occupied, the three of you can go up the back stairs and get Tom.'

'I wish I knew the layout of the place,' said Frankie. 'We could end up getting totally lost.'

'I'll show you the entrance that'll take you to the back stairs,' said Rhea. 'Just go on up to the fourth floor. You want Corridor D. Turn left at the end, past the lifts, and you'll know where you are. You'll recognize it from there.'

Jack frowned. She seemed to know a lot about the design of the hospital. He looked up and saw Rhea's eyes watching him in the narrow mirror. The light made them look dark brown, although he was sure he remembered them as blue.

'I know the place pretty well,' she said, as though reading his thoughts. 'A friend of mine was laid-up there a while back.'

'We're here,' said Frankie.

Rhea guided the car in through the front entrance of the hospital. The frontage was ablaze with light in the growing night.

Rhea slowed the car right down. 'OK,' she said. 'I'll park over there where it's less brightly lit. You need to go that way.' She indicated a route down the left side of the main building. 'It's the second door you come to. If I'm not here when you get back, wait for me, right?' She looked around at them. 'It's going to be fine, OK? Everything will be just fine.'

Rhea drove to the darkened area she had indicated and they got out of the car.

Rhea walked towards the main entrance.

The three friends skirted the carpark and headed down the side of the hospital. No one paid them any attention.

Something is wrong. It pounded in Jack's brain. Like a hammer. Over and over. *Wrong.* He stopped and looked back the way they had come.

'Don't just stand there,' Regan hissed. 'Get with it, man! We don't have all night.'

Frankie looked concernedly into his troubled face. 'What is it, Jack?'

He shook his head. 'There's something not right about this,' he said hesitantly.

'What? Do you think Tom's already been—'

'No. No, it's not that.' Jack screwed up his eyes. *Wrong! Wrong Wrong!* It throbbed in his head. But what was wrong?

'Come on, guys,' Regan insisted.

'It's something to do with Rhea,' said Jack.

Regan stared at him. 'Like what?'

'I don't know. She's too . . . too . . .' Come on! Pinpoint the thought. 'Too easygoing about all this. What if she intends to just stroll in there and tell Dr Fairfax what we're up to? Isn't that what any adult would do? Really? What if she's just playing along with us?'

Regan's eyes narrowed. 'Nasty thought there, Jack,' she said.

'But it would explain why she hasn't asked us why we think Dr Fairfax wants to hurt Tom,' said Frankie. 'If she hasn't believed us right from the word go.'

'In that case, we'd better get our backsides in

gear,' said Regan. She turned and ran for the door. 'Move it, people!' she called back. 'Regan's Raiders are go!'

Frankie and Jack raced after her. She was right. If Rhea was going to betray them to the hospital authorities, they needed to act quickly.

There wasn't a moment to lose.

CHAPTER SEVENTEEN

Rescued by Rhea

J ack was the first into the room.

Regan and Frankie crowded in behind him.

Tom's bed was empty.

The bedcovers were thrown back. There was a magazine open face-down on the floor.

Too late!

'Now what?' Regan breathed.

Jack's hands clenched into rock-hard fists. They were too late. Tom had already been taken.

'I don't know.' Jack was trying to keep calm. 'Let me think.'

'Maybe we could . . .' Frankie stared around the room, as if hoping to find some clue as to what had happened in there. 'Maybe . . . if . . .' Her voice trailed away.

What could they do?

'Hello, guys, bit late for visiting, isn't it?'

They spun at the sound of the voice.

'Tom! You absolute, total and utter idiot!' howled Regan. Tom was standing there in the corridor right behind them. Dressed in his pyjamas. 'What the heck do you think you're playing at?'

His eyebrows shot up. 'I needed to go to the loo, if it's any of your busi-*yoik*!' Jack's arm stretched out over Regan's shoulder and Tom was yanked unceremoniously into the room.

Frankie shut the door.

'Here,' Tom complained, jerking himself loose and glaring at his brother. 'What's the big idea?'

'Get dressed,' Jack ordered. He ran to the bedside cabinet. He opened the door and pulled out jeans, a shirt, shoes, underwear. Fresh clothes brought in for Tom by his mother. 'Get these on – now!'

'Wait a minute . . .'

'Tom, there's no time,' Frankie said urgently. 'Just do it.'

'Regan – check the corridor,' said Jack.

Regan opened the door a crack and peered out. 'All clear so far,' she said. Tom was standing in the middle of the floor, staring at them with his mouth open.

'Will someone explain what this is all about?' he said.

'It's about Dr Bludworth,' said Jack.

Tom went rigid, his eyes circular.

'Bludworth . . .' he gaped. He shuddered and seemed about to fall. 'He . . . has . . . poisoned us . . . all . . .'

Frankie darted forwards and threw her arms around him. 'Tom! Stay with us! Hey! Hey! Listen to me, Tom. Don't fade out on us now.' She lightly slapped his cheek. 'Tom!'

Tom's eyes came back into focus. 'Stop hitting me! I'm not well.'

'Get dressed or we'll take you out like you are,' Jack said.

'Are you potty? I'm not changing in front of these two!' Tom declared.

Regan glanced around at him from her lookout post at the door. 'Wear 'em or eat 'em!' she said. 'Your choice.'

'You lot had better have a good explanation for this,' Tom muttered as he grabbed the jeans out of Jack's hand and shoved a pajama'd leg into them. 'In fact, it's going to have to be the most brilliant expla—'

'Sufferin' cats!' Regan hissed, returning her eye to the crack in the door. 'It's Fairfax. At the end of the corridor. He's coming this way.'

'Rhea?' asked Frankie.

'No. Just him. What do we do, guys? Barricade ourselves in here?'

'No!' said Jack. 'We run!'

He bundled the rest of Tom's clothes up under his arm. Tom was still fastening his jeans as Jack grabbed him and towed him to the door.

'Count of three,' hissed Regan. 'One . . . two . . . three . . . *go*!' She threw the door open and the four of them went hurtling out into the corridor. Even Tom seemed to have realized that this was serious.

'Hey! You! Stop!' They ignored the startled yell from the far end of the corridor. They had a fifteen-metre head-start on Fairfax.

They pelted along the corridor. As they came to the bend that led into Corridor D, Frankie glanced back. Fairfax was running after them, his white coat billowing, his face thunderous.

They hit the stairs.

It was a wild scramble. Tom's head was whirling. The stairwell spun. He stumbled. Regan caught hold of his wrist and saved him from falling.

They came to the final flight. Frankie jumped the last five treads and threw herself at the door.

Rhea's car was parked right across their path.

Frankie flung her arms out, trying to warn the others.

Their escape route was blocked!

Rhea leaned over in the car and thrust the passenger door open.

'Quick!' Rhea called. 'Get in. They couldn't find Fairfax for me.'

'He's right behind us!' Frankie panted. She jerked the car's back door open and the four friends tumbled in. There was a grinding sound as Rhea searched for the right gear.

The car jerked forwards. Jack slammed the back door. Rhea plunged them across the carpark. Through the rear window, Regan saw Dr Fairfax appear at the side entrance.

The car bounced out onto the road. Rhea spun the wheel and everyone was thrown about like peas in a rattle.

'Whoo-ee!' Regan squealed as Tom and Jack nearly flattened her against the inside of the door. 'Way to go, Rhea! Destruction Derby!'

'I hope not,' said Rhea. She took a moment to glance back at her tumbled passengers. 'Hello, Tom. Everyone OK?'

'Fine,' Jack gasped, clamping his hands on the back of Frankie's seat. 'That was close!'

Two or three fast corners on and Rhea slowed the car down to a more sensible speed.

She flicked a glance at Jack. 'Where are we going?'

'Good question,' said Frankie. She looked around at Jack. 'Where *are* we going?'

Jack had been so wrapped up in getting Tom out of the hospital, that he hadn't given any thought to what they would do next.

'Tell you what,' said Rhea. 'How about we go back to my place while you think about it? Fairfax won't be able to find you there.'

'Yes.' Jack nodded, grateful for the breathing space that this solution allowed. 'Yes, that'd be great.' He pushed the rest of Tom's clothes into his brother's lap. 'There you go. You can finish dressing now.'

'Thanks a bunch,' Tom said. 'What's going on?'

Regan let out a breathless bark of laughter. 'You want the whole story, or just the edited highlights?'

Jack glanced at Rhea. 'I'm not sure we should talk about it right this minute,' he said. He accepted he'd been wrong about Rhea's motives for helping them, but letting her in on the full madness of their situation was another matter entirely.

'Oh, come on!' Tom exclaimed.

'Excuse me for butting in,' Rhea said, 'but I've gone along with you people so far, no questions asked. I think maybe it's time for some explanations. Don't you?'

'She's right,' said Frankie. 'We'll have to tell her, Jack. She might even be able to help.'

The car rushed on through the night.

Jack nodded.

Frankie was right. The story needed to be told.

Tom's head lolled against Jack's shoulder. His eyes were open, but they were fixed – staring at nothing.

It was difficult to tell how much of Jack's account he had taken in. He seemed to be drifting in and out of awareness.

An intense silence came down after Jack had finished speaking.

Rhea had parked the car some minutes before, but no one had moved. She had switched the motor off. The only light filtered down from a street-lamp. On one side of the road was a square patch of green, hemmed by black rails; on the other, tall pale terraced houses.

Regan raised her eyebrows and looked at Rhea. 'Pretty far-out, huh?'

Rhea shook her head. Slowly. 'It's not the kind of thing you get told every day,' she said.

'But it is true,' said Frankie.

Rhea nodded. 'I haven't said otherwise.'

'What I don't get,' Regan said, looking at Rhea. 'Is how come you haven't been chased by rats or jumped on by people whose faces are falling off – or . . . or anything!' She looked at her friends. 'Why just us?'

Frankie frowned. 'That's true,' she said. 'You were there, just like we were.'

'Maybe I'm immune,' Rhea said. 'Who knows?' She shrugged. 'Shall we go on up? I think I could do with a drink.'

'Yeah, I could murder a coke right now,' said Regan.

'That's not quite what I had in mind,' said Rhea.

They got out of the car. Tom was conscious but seemed to be in a stupor. Between them, Jack and Frankie guided him up the steps to the front door of the house. A dozen or more bells were ranged down the side of the door.

Rhea let them in. They followed her up the stairs, to a landing with three doors leading off it.

'It's a bit of a tip,' Rhea said, as she opened the door to her flat.

Rhea's flat was small and chaotic – as if someone was either in the process of moving in, or moving out. There were cardboard boxes, piles of books and oddments, an open suitcase spilling clothes.

'Go on through into the living room,' Rhea said. 'I'll make us something to drink. Who wants what? Coffee? Tea? Orange juice? I think there's some cans.'

'Coke, if you've got it,' said Regan. 'Otherwise a vodka martini will do just fine. Shaken but not stirred.'

'Yeah. Nice one!' Rhea laughed as she headed for the skinny kitchen.

Regan blinked after her. 'I wasn't joking,' she muttered.

They steered Tom into the jumble of the living room. Frankie cleared some stuff off an armchair and Tom slumped into it.

Jack looked anxiously at him. He was very pale.

Then Frankie said something that lifted the hair at the back of Jack's neck.

'You know, I'd swear Rhea's eyes were *blue* before. They're brown now.'

Regan was nosing through a row of CDs on a shelf. 'That's no big mystery,' she said. 'Tinted contact lenses would do that. Maybe she fancied a change. Aha! Way to go, Rhea!'

She grinned around at them. 'She has the new

Trancebop album. It's brilliant to the max.' She looked around for a player. 'Jack? Where you going?'

'Just to help Rhea,' said Jack.

A cramped corridor led off from the living room to the small kitchen. The kitchen door was half-ajar. For some reason, Rhea hadn't put the light on in there.

Jack paced silently along the carpet. The dark slot of the doorway opened up to him like a hungry mouth. The feeling that he was approaching something dangerous began to sing in his ears. Every hair stood erect on his body, as though a warning thrill of electricity was running through him.

He swallowed. A hollowness beat up under his ribs.

Something terrible. Old. Dredged up from the dead past. Congested with vengeance.

Jack stood silently at the door. He could see Rhea's dark shape, leaning forwards, as though working at something hidden by shadows.

Her head was limned with a faint greenish glow, like a halo of sickness. Like the miasma that had been said to cling to the skulls of plague-bearers.

And there was a smell. An awful smell.

Fear gripped Jack and his head reeled.

It was all he could do to stay on his feet.

CHAPTER EIGHTEEN

Dr Bludworth

A cackle of laughter from Regan in the living room drew Jack out of the sucking darkness.

'Well, look-ee what I found!'

Some discovery back there had amused her. The distraction brought Jack back to his senses. He focused his mind, beating down the terror that was threatening to swamp him.

Slowly, cautiously, he reached in through the kitchen doorway, feeling alongside the wall for a light-switch.

He found it. With a soft click the room was bathed in light.

Rhea turned, hissing, her face twisted with mal-evolence. Five glasses were ranged on the worksurface. She was holding a small green earthen-ware flask. Thick, yellow liquid was draining into one of the glasses. Jack knew instantly the nature of that vile liquid: it was poison!

Rhea was poisoning their drinks.

His appalling blunder was revealed to him in a flash. He had sensed that the vengeful spirit of Dr

Bludworth was at large – but he had totally misunder-stood the direction from which the danger would strike. Dr Fairfax wasn't the vessel into which Blud-worth had poured his evil. It was Rhea!

'No!' Rhea's voice was a ragged howl. 'No! I shall not be thwarted a second time!' She flung the flask at Jack.

He ducked back. The flask cracked off the wall, spilling the bile-coloured poison.

Jack snatched at the door handle. If he could hold the door closed – contain the thing in there – maybe it would give the others a chance to escape.

But he was too slow. Rhea bounded forwards and wrenched the door out of his hand. She came over him like an avalanche, sending him crumpling to the ground. He tried to grab her legs, but she trampled and kicked at him in a fury.

'What the – Jack!' He glimpsed Frankie's face at the living room door.

'She's Bludworth!' Jack shouted. 'It's her!'

Rhea lurched forwards along the corridor. Alarm whitened Frankie's face. She backed away, shouting a warning into the room. Jack scrambled to his feet. He stumbled after Rhea.

Rhea burst into the living room. Jack saw her strike out at Frankie. He saw Frankie fall.

Rhea – or the dreadful thing that inhabited Rhea – was snarling and shouting.

Then Jack heard Regan's voice.

'One more step, buster! Just one more step and I'll whack you into the middle of next week! Believe it!'

Jack staggered into the doorway. Regan was standing guard over Tom. She was holding a hockey stick in both hands at shoulder height, poised, balanced on the balls of her feet, ready to take a swing at Rhea.

Rhea stooped, panting, in the middle of the floor, glaring at the defiant girl.

Tom was staring at Rhea in utter terror. His face was grey.

Rhea's voice grated. 'Will . . . come here, my boy. Will Hilliard – come to me . . . do not fear me. I shall not harm you.'

'You stay put, man,' Regan hissed.

But Tom was straining to get up out of the chair.

'Tom!' Jack shouted. 'Listen to me! You're not Will Hilliard. You're Tom Christmas! Hoi! Tom! Listen to me!'

'He lies,' Rhea snarled. She held her hands out to Tom. 'Come . . . I shall take you to your mother and father. They wish to see you, Will. And your brothers and sisters. Would you abandon them?'

Rhea's voice was compelling. Hypnotic. Against all sense, Tom felt his willpower ebbing away. He rose unsteadily to his feet, his face blank. His mouth loose.

'Tom!' Frankie's voice. 'Don't believe her – him – it! Listen to Jack!'

'Lies!' snarled Rhea. 'Wicked, damnable lies.'

Regan gave a practice swipe with the hockey stick. Rhea bridled back.

'Tom!' shouted Jack. 'You've been ill. You swallowed a load of filthy water. Don't you remember? At the dig.'

'You have to remember!' cried Frankie. 'Tom – you must!'

'No . . .' Tom whispered. 'I'm . . . Will . . .'

'Nuts you are!' growled Regan.

Rhea made a move forwards. Regan swung the stick again. Whoosh! It clove, solid and menacing, through the air between them.

'Now just you listen to me, Tom,' Regan snapped. Her eyes never left Rhea. 'You are not Will Hilliard, no matter what this dingbat tells you. You're Tom Christmas, and if you don't pull yourself together right now, I'm gonna shove this stick up your nose and yank it out through your ear! And then I'm gonna bang your head on the floor until you get a grip! Get the picture?' She glowered at Rhea. 'Face it, pal. This ain't gonna happen.'

Tom's face changed, as though some choked-off part of him had broken loose. His eyes swam into focus.

'Oh! Crikey!' He stared around him in a daze. 'Wha . . .?'

Rhea screamed.

Tom toppled backwards into the armchair, limb-loose and frog-eyed.

The scream grew in intensity. Rhea's body writhed. The scream split, the pitch separating, extending simultaneously to a higher and a lower tone. Like two voices screaming in unison. A woman's voice. And a man's voice.

A greenish mist gathered around the contorting body.

Regan took a step backwards – her eyes reflecting the nauseous glow.

Jack hung on to the door-frame. Frankie kicked herself back until she hit against the wall.

The stench gagged them all.

Something began to happen to the twisting,

howling shape. It seemed to become deformed, as though melting. And then one part of the shape fell away, collapsing to the floor like a discarded husk. The high-pitched voice bubbled away to nothing.

A tall, dark figure stood where Rhea had been. It was wrapped in the diseased green miasma. A man. Wearing a raven cloak. His distorted face was lined and rugged. His hair grey. His eyes a brown that was almost black.

It was Dr Bludworth.

He flailed at the enveloping mist and bellowed in terror.

The hockey stick fell out of Regan's hands.

The man staggered, beating at the mist with his hands.

He fell across the room. Regan sprang out of his way. But he seemed to be unaware of her. He drummed his hands on the window. Shouting.

'No! Do not leave me here! Not *here*!'

He turned, his eyes wild, his face wrung with despair.

He ran towards Jack, the pitiless mist swirling about him. His fists rained down on Jack's chest. Jack felt nothing.

The doctor fell to his knees.

'*Help me*!'

But he wasn't seeing Jack. He was seeing only an implacably locked and barred door.

'I shall *die*!'

He crawled to the centre of the room, twisting in his torment.

His face began to fall apart. Livid red weals flowered over his flesh. His eyes sank deep into their sockets. A purple blush spread over his face. Raw lesions opened on his skin. Blood dribbled from the corner of his mouth.

He gave one last, croaking cry, and then collapsed onto his face.

The mist swirled and gathered.

And then it faded.

The dark hump of the fallen man began to dissolve. To liquefy and soften and run into the carpet, until not even a stain was left.

Regan swallowed hard, her eyes stapled to the section of carpet where Bludworth had perished. 'Jeez,' she whispered. 'I really wish I hadn't seen that.'

Rhea groaned and moved.

She lifted herself on one elbow. Her head hung heavily.

'Oh! Thank God!' she gasped. 'He's gone! He's gone at last!'

The sweet breath of summer flowers flowed through the room.

All the evil and the misery and the despair had departed.

A week passed.

The four friends were in Darryl's attic. At least that was a place where they could talk freely. Who else but Darryl could even begin to believe the things that had happened to them?

Not Rhea. She had no memory of anything that had happened between that rainy afternoon in the black cellar, and waking up on her living room carpet with the four friends staring down at her. She put it down to stress. Overwork.

The friends had come to the decision not to fill

in the blanks. Rhea would be appalled to learn that she had tried to kill Tom. It was much better to leave her in ignorance of the past few days. Much better all round not to tell her about what Bludworth had almost made her do.

Explaining the abduction of Tom from his hospital bed had been tricky. Jack, Frankie and Regan had taken him back there the same evening. Dr Fairfax had already called Tom and Jack's parents. They had been angry and frantic with worry. Tom had told them that he'd panicked. Claustrophobia, or something like that. It was all his fault. The others thought they were helping him. Sorry.

There might have been repercussions, if not for the fact that Tom's mysterious symptoms had vanished that same night. He was home by lunchtime the following day. Good as new.

Darryl had wanted to hear the entire story. Of course, Rhea – or Bludworth, as they now knew – had made no attempt to contact Darryl that stupefying night. His one desire was to destroy the boy who had been the cause of his death. His hope had been that the three friends would give him access to Tom – to Will Hilliard.

'We didn't figure it at the time,' Regan said. 'Heck, why should we? But that was why Rhea kept visiting Tom. She wanted to wipe him out.'

'But there were always other people there,' added Tom. 'Fortunately.'

'I wish you wouldn't keep saying *she*,' said Frankie. 'It was him – Bludworth – not Rhea. She had no say in the matter.'

'We think the bottle of cherry cola she brought in for Tom was probably poisoned,' said Jack. 'That's why the lid didn't pop. She'd opened it when she put the poison in.'

'Lucky I spotted it,' said Tom. 'Not everyone would have noticed a small thing like that.'

'Yeah,' Regan drawled. 'And not everyone would have been down in that big wet cellar sucking on a drainpipe in the first place. Most people got more brains. It's you messing up like a total dweez that got us into trouble, man. We could've all wound up dead.'

'Oh! That's right. Blame me!' Tom exclaimed. 'I suppose you think I did it on purpose?'

'No, I think you did it cos you don't have the savvy of a retarded newt—'

'Excuse me!' Darryl's voice cut sharply across the budding argument. 'War-free zone, people!' he laughed. 'Anyhow, I've got some information that you might be interested to hear. About the bones from the plague pit.'

'Oh, yes,' said Jack. 'I was wondering about them. What happened down there?'

'Well, Professor Paulson and his people worked in the cellar for quite a few days,' said Darryl. 'Once they had all the bones sorted and photographed, each body was given its own reference number. Then the bodies were bagged up and sent off to a specialist to determine the sex and age at death.'

'How do they do that?' asked Tom.

'The shape of the pelvis can usually show whether the body was male or female,' said Darryl. 'And the length of the bones helps determine the age of the victim. It's a complex procedure. It can take quite a while.'

'And what happens after the specialists have finished?' asked Regan.

'They'll write a report on each set of bones,' said Darryl. 'And then the bodies will be taken to consecrated ground and given a proper re-burial.'

Tom nodded. 'So, I suppose that'll be the end of it.'

'That's not quite the end,' said Darryl with a wry smile. 'There is something else that might interest you. Something I dug up, you might say.'

'Is it about the Hilliards?' asked Frankie. 'Have you found out something about them?'

Darryl nodded. 'I logged into the history department's files in the University,' he said. 'They've got loads of local stuff on computer. Including copies of records that go right back to the seventeenth century.'

'Did you find out anything about Will?' Tom asked. 'Did he get the plague?'

'Yes. The on-file patient records of the old pest house show someone called W. Hilliard being treated there.'

Tom hung his head. 'Oh. I thought so.' It was a dismal thought that the boy who had shared his head for those few strange days had died in the pest house. 'That explains the dreams I had about being ill with plague.'

'Not so fast,' Darryl said with a smile. 'The records show he recovered!'

'Whoo!' Regan crowed. 'Good for Will!'

'The rest of his family were dead, though, weren't they?' said Jack. 'Poor kid!'

'They were,' said Darryl. 'But parish records from the time show that a boy by the name of Will Hilliard was adopted into a Lychford family soon after the epidemic fizzled out.'

'He was adopted?' said Tom. 'Hey, not bad.'

A slow, crooked grin spread over Darryl's face. 'And the records go on to show that Will grew up to be a doctor.' His eyes twinkled behind his horn-rimmed glasses. 'Anyone want to hazard a guess at the name of the people who adopted him?'

There was a brief, puzzled silence.

'Ohmigosh!' breathed Frankie. 'I know what you're going to say! It was Fairfax, wasn't it! He grew up to be Dr Fairfax!'

Darryl nodded. 'And the Fairfax family have provided doctors in Lychford ever since.' He grinned like a crocodile. 'Nice twist, eh?'

'Nice?' Tom gasped. 'It's totally and utterly brilliant!'

Afterword

Bubonic, Pneumonic and Septicemic Plague are the three forms of a disease which has existed for over three thousand years. Recorded epidemics in China go back to 224 BC. The disease is caused by the bacillus *Yersina pestis* – a particularly unpleasant little germ carried in the stomachs of rat-fleas.

Bubonic Plague is fatal in 30 to 75 per cent of cases. Pneumonic plague is fatal in 95 per cent of cases. Septicemic plague is nearly always fatal.

The victims turn a purple colour in their last hours. In the Middle Ages, it was this symptom that gave the disease the name the Black Death.

Plague is transmitted by flea-bites. The most common carrier of the disease is the rat flea *Xenopsylla cheopis*, which lives on brown rats, but which will indiscriminately bite humans given the opportunity. This usually happens when the rat-host drops dead and the fleas find themselves temporarily homeless.

The Plague is a big killer: the Black Death wiped out about a third of the population of Great Britain in the fourteenth century. Another epidemic caused havoc in the 1600s. One of its most notorious occurrences is still referred to as the Great Plague of London. At least 70,000 people died in the city alone in the years 1664–65.

A common misconception is that the Great Fire of London brought the Great Plague to an end. It didn't – although the new housing, and the improved sanitation that appeared after the fire, probably helped to stop the plague coming back.

It is also generally believed that the bodies of the victims of the Great Plague of London were hurled in heaps into mass graves – into plague pits. This is not true. Archaeological research has shown that the bodies were laid out in neat rows and that the victims were given as decent a burial as their overwhelming numbers allowed.

Quack doctors did peddle 'cures' such as plague water – and there is evidence that looting and plundering of bodies and homes did take place, although it was far from widespread.

The last big outbreak of Plague began in China in 1894. It spread westwards into Africa and got as far east as San Francisco in the USA before it burned itself out. In 1950 the World Health Organization set up plague control programs throughout the world. The most recent outbreaks of the disease happened in India in 1994.

Plague is still around.

Allan Frewin Jones
Dark Paths 1:
THE WICKER MAN

Roll up, roll up, for the human sacrifice!

It's May Day, and every year in the village of Bodin Summerley
a May Queen and Jack-in-the-Green are chosen to lead the
festivities. OK, so maybe it is kind of spooky that the old
traditions are based on pagan sacrifices – but hey! These days
it's just harmless fun, right?

But Regan, Frankie, Jack and Tom are wrong. Horribly,
hideously wrong. For the ancient power of the old gods, buried
deep for centuries, is gathering force again. And now it demands
a new victim. This year, when the Wicker Man is burned on
the bonfire, it will contain a living boy . . .

Books in the DARK PATHS series available from Macmillan

The prices shown below are correct at the time of going to press. However, Macmillan Publishers reserve the right to show new retail prices on covers which may differ from those previously advertised.

ALLAN FREWIN JONES

1. The Wicker Man		0 330 36806 0	£3.99
2. The Plague Pit		0 330 36807 9	£3.99
3. Unquiet Graves	*Jan. 1999*	0 330 36808 7	£3.99
4. The Phantom Airman	*Mar. 1999*	0 330 36809 5	£3.99
5. The Wreckers	*May 1999*	0 330 36810 9	£3.99
6. The Monk's Curse	*July 1999*	0 330 36811 7	£3.99

All Macmillan titles can be ordered at your local bookshop or are available by post from:

**Book Service by Post
PO Box 29, Douglas, Isle of Man IM99 1BQ**

Credit cards accepted. For details:
Telephone: 01624 675137
Fax: 01624 670923
E-mail: bookshop@enterprise.net

Free postage and packing in the UK.
Overseas customers: add £1 per book (paperback)
and £3 per book (hardback).